MW01277964

Faraj!

A Space of Possibility

Kira Van Deusen

for Nazila — with best wishes!
Kira Van Deusen

FriesenPress

Suite 300 - 990 Fort St
Victoria, BC, V8V 3K2
Canada

www.friesenpress.com

Copyright © 2016 by Kira Van Deusen
First Edition — 2016

Illustrations by Mahdiyar Biazi and Shamin Zahabioun

Permissions for use of previously published material are on page 167.

All rights reserved. No part of this publication may be reproduced in any form, or by any means, electronic or mechanical, including photocopying, recording, or any information browsing, storage, or retrieval system, without permission in writing from FriesenPress.

ISBN
978-1-4602-8681-4 (Paperback)
978-1-4602-8682-1 (eBook)

1. FICTION, ROMANCE, HISTORICAL, MEDIEVAL

Distributed to the trade by The Ingram Book Company

Faraj!

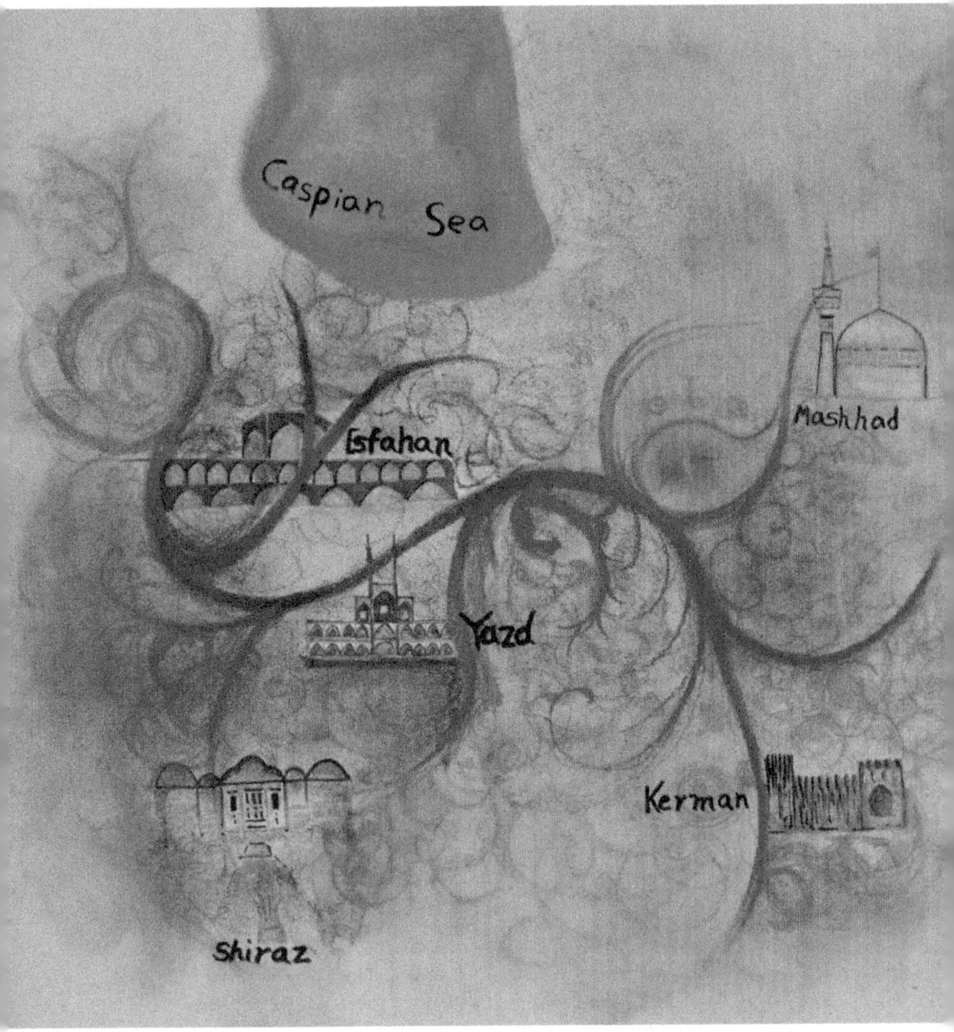
Caspian Sea
Mashhad
Esfahan
Yazd
Kerman
Shiraz

Introduction

Invited by my friends Fleur Talebi and Hossein Mashreghi, I made my first trip to Iran in the spring of 2012. These generous people live most of the time in Vancouver and return regularly to the city of Mashhad in northeastern Iran.

We went on a long road trip, making a circle through central Iran. People we talked with in villages and cities were going about their lives, happy to acquaint an outsider with their long and fascinating history, magnificent art and architecture, places of natural beauty, mystic poetry, delicious food and legendary hospitality. They showed me the human and multicultural face of Iran, beyond stereotypes created by our fear-mongering media.

We visited Bajestan, where my friends had spent childhood summers. Hossein spoke of it as a village, but it looked more like a small city to me; he admitted that the population was now about 20,000. Like everywhere else in Iran, the population has grown immensely since the revolution in 1979, a growth encouraged by the government.

We turned off a busy street with shops and restaurants, and made a phone call that brought a caretaker to the gate. Hossein's family owns the place, although no one lives there now. Once down a short driveway, we felt we were in the country, surrounded by fields and beige mud-brick houses.

While Fleur and I sat, chatting in the sun, Hossein visited with neighbours. At that time in 2012, sanctions against Iran had just begun. Were people talking about that in Bajestan? No. Were they debating the pros and cons of their country's controversial nuclear program? No. Were they talking about their recent federal elections? No. They were talking about water, concerned there would be a shortage that summer. And indeed, since then, water has continued to be a serious concern in Iran. By 2015, groundwater had become dangerously low and rivers had dried up.

Most of the areas we passed through in central Iran were very dry, at least in the eyes of a person from the rainforests of Canada's west coast. I called it "variations on a theme of desert." Soon though, I saw distinctions. There were true sandy deserts and bare, jagged rocky mountains. One of these was sliced open; inside its brown coat was pink marble, destined most likely for floors in Europe. Then there was the *sahrā*. I know of no place in Canada like this cross between desert and prairie — often bare, with hills, rocky outcrops and patches of thorn bushes.

I also saw evidence of the soil's fertility when nourished with water and became interested in ancient water systems. When we visited the Yazd Water Museum, I learned about the underground water channels (*qanāts*), how the channels were built and maintained, the various containers used to carry water, and ingenious ways water was stored and used for drinking, washing and air conditioning during the very hot summers. The *qanāt* system goes back at least 2,000 years. As many as 50,000 water channels were still in use in 2012, despite the cities having more modern systems.

At the museum, Fleur chatted with a man who had worked in the *qanāts* his whole life. She expressed her admiration for his willingness to risk his life daily so that others could have water. Dangerous work, since *qanāts* sometimes collapsed. Those workers wore white, the colour used for burying the dead, to show their acceptance of the risk.

Faraj!

Countless travellers have passed through Yazd. It is said people have lived in that location for 7,000 years. For centuries Yazd marked the crossroads of several major trade routes through the Iranian deserts. It likely gained importance because of its access to water from nearby mountains. The city evolved as part of the Silk Road, a system of trade routes stretching from China to Europe and North Africa.

In those days, people came to Yazd from far and near. There were Arabs in long white robes and white turbans with black ties, and women from Iran's south coast wearing pants with embroidered cuffs and leather masks to protect their faces from the sun. Travellers from farther east and even Europe might be selling anything from silks to cooking pots. Commodities such as silk, porcelain, mirrors, umbrellas, medicines, paper, tea and rice could have come to Iran all the way from China.

In turn, seeds, grapes, onions and carrots, woollen rugs and blankets, camels and other animals moved in the other direction. Some products didn't make the entire journey but were traded along the way through Central Asia, contributing to the wealth of tribal empires.

Despite being quite isolated from other urban centres, Yazd was, and still is, the centre of the Zoroastrian religion in Iran. Travel to cities such as Esfahān and Shirāz to the west, Rasht in the north, Mashhad in the northeast, or ports on the Persian Gulf to the south could take weeks. There was always danger of bandits, storms and wild animals — even lions and tigers — along the way.

Rural villages outside of Yazd were largely populated by Zoroastrians, mostly farmers. Villages closest to the city were gradually absorbed as the urban population increased. Others lie farther away in the mountains. To the south is Cham, with a cypress tree thousands of years old and dramatic Towers of Silence set against a backdrop of rocky mountains. Farther in the direction of Shirāz is Taft, with a stunning mountain in the shape of an eagle. To the north, Sharifābād long held the sacred Zoroastrian flame until it was moved to Yazd.

The village in this story is fictional, based on these and other places. With apologies to the beautiful city, I have taken liberties with the geography of Yazd and the village where Ābtin's family lives, making distances more walkable than they are in real life. My friends and I rode in Hossein's red Peugeot, past deserted caravanserais and modern roadside rest areas that provide water faucets and small mosques, as well as places for picnics. We listened to music from the archives of a popular pre-revolutionary radio program that Fleur had recorded for the trip. The music seemed to connect us to the landscape. Munching fresh dates and pistachios grown in the irrigated land, I looked out the windows to see saffron, almonds, oranges and lemons growing by the side of the road.

Fleur told me a story about a man from Yazd who made a long journey during a year of water shortage. He had numerous adventures, finally arriving at the Caspian Sea. Seeing all that water must have been as amazing for him as seeing the desert was for me. I felt an immediate kinship with him. When he returned home, he found his words were inadequate to convey everything he had seen and so he wove his experience into a carpet.

Although the story was short, it stuck with me. I wondered who the man was, why he left home and what he learned. After returning to Canada, I was inspired to tell his story more fully as *The Carpet Weaver's Apprentice*. While on the road, the man dreamed of a girl back home and soon I was telling her story too, *Mitrā — the One Who Waited*. Finally I decided to write the two stories down and find out what happened next.

I've been a professional storyteller for twenty-five years. It all began with my fascination with indigenous cultures in Siberia, where I regularly travelled over fifteen years, gathering stories and participating in the cultural revival that happened after the fall of the Soviet Union. I came back, told those stories frequently and wrote several non-fiction books about the whole experience. That led to a brief but rewarding trip to the Canadian north, recording forty Inuit elders telling one of their great epics — the story of the hero Kiviuq.

At home, a group of storytellers began to gather once a year to tell an epic, each time from a different culture. This continues to be a wonderful way to connect with multicultural communities in Vancouver. Twice we have told Persian stories, which led me to study the language and culture of that great nation. When I realized that many of Iran's nomadic people are culturally and linguistically related to some of the people I met in Russia, it sent shivers down my spine.

As I started this writing project, it soon became clear to me that writing a story is quite different from telling one and that writing fiction is different from writing non-fiction. One thing they all have in common is the process of approaching a new culture and trying to understand its depth.

Story listeners have felt that my oral stories speak of experience that transcends time — the events could happen today since many things have not changed over the centuries. The written story requires certain details that oral storytelling leaves to the inner eye of the listener. For readers, it's not enough that the story is set "long ago." Most want to know more precisely when it happened so they can orient themselves in time and space.

What do the characters look like? We storytellers rarely describe their appearance unless there's a significant reason to do so. Readers look for these cues. Details that are carried by the storyteller's voice and gesture in an oral story must be made explicit in a written one.

As far as cultural setting goes, there is much to learn. Most of us are familiar with Persian rugs, and possibly food and music.

However, there is a wealth of history, customs, landscapes and rules that reveal themselves only as we get to know each other better. Although many of these are portrayed in the story itself, I felt that too much detail could create a diversion from the plot. For those who are interested, details about the historical period and the two religions that play such an influential role in the story are explored in the information section at the end of the book.

I was occasionally frustrated, realizing that certain things couldn't have happened as I imagined them. These were dilemmas of their own time and place, and I came to see that the characters would find their own solutions if I listened to them. For example, a woman should not go out alone, which meant that Mitrā's sister began to play an important role whenever the two went out together. Parties were gender-segregated, so I had to find a new way for the bad guy to see Mitrā for the first time. The dress code provided both challenges and opportunities.

It's possible that people like those in my story were just as frustrated by what I perceived as restrictions. On the other hand, they might have seen them as "just the way things are" or even as positively beneficial — I had to widen my perspective. It's also possible that historians don't tell us everything about the human heart and inevitable exceptions to the rules. Societies shift, for better or for worse, occasionally at the insistence of visionaries and lovers. I have tried to balance getting the details of cultural history right with being true to my characters' vision.

Speaking in contemporary western terms, we could say that Mitrā and Ābtin are being true to themselves. In their time and place, the same behaviours might have seemed individualistic, selfish or even dangerous and immoral. Following their hearts forced them to make difficult choices that involved their families as well as themselves. Finding a more acceptable way could have included following time-honoured coming-of-age rituals and engaging in community service rather than social justice and the arts, especially if the latter choices reached beyond their own family and community.

Today, Iranians of diverse religions often have warm friendships, whereas a hundred years ago this was not often the case. Nonetheless, down through the ages, people have lived comfortably beside neighbours of different religions and classes. More often than not, separations and wars have come at the hands of hostile governments or other forms of leadership, and often for economic and political reasons. Just look at Christians and Muslims in Bosnia, or Muslims and Jews in Israel and Palestine. I've also experienced this with ethnic Europeans and indigenous people in small Russian villages, and among various cultures in urban Canadian schools.

I wish you interesting conversations.

Now on with the story!

1
Mitrā
Fall 1662

Dust swirled, raised by the passing camels. It found its way inside Mitrā's clothes and into her ears. She waited impatiently, coughing and glancing out of nearly closed eyes until the dust finally settled. The caravan disappeared into the distance, the sound of its bells a faint echo. A breeze picked up her long red skirts and the all-encompassing white shawl she wore whenever she went outside. Since no one was around, she uncovered her face to enjoy the fresh air.

Mitrā stood on the road going northwest out of her hometown of Yazd beside the Towers of Silence. They loomed large, dominating the landscape. Round and tall, made of mud-brick and stone, they sat tall on natural formations of rough, reddish-brown rock with a man-made pathway spiralling to the top.

The road led from the city's brown brick houses and bustling bazaar, through several small villages, past the imposing Towers and across barren lands into the mountains. Travellers spent weeks on the road to arrive at the glittering capital city of Esfahān. Mitrā didn't know anyone who had gone that far and come back to tell of it.

Caravans came and went with tales of a bridge with thirty-three arches crossing the Zayandeh river. Who could imagine a river that wide? Most Yazdis had seen little more than a mountain creek that dried up in the summer. In Esfahān you might even see the Shāh riding past the golden-domed mosques, wearing so much gold it hurt your eyes. The world beyond the mountains was a mystery, filled with danger and romance.

Ābtin had disappeared into that mystery.

Would he ever come back? He had left by that same road in early summer and now the weather was cooling as fall advanced. The waiting made her restless.

Why did she think Ābtin might arrive from that direction? There were many roads leading in and out of Yazd. He had travelled with a caravan for safety and company, the camel train leaving late in the day to avoid the extreme heat of the Yazd summer. Mitrā had crept out of the house when everyone was resting and walked past the bazaar to the caravanserai. She stayed hidden so he wouldn't see her tears as the camels started their long journey.

They had already said goodbye. "I'm going to see if I can better my fortunes somewhere else," he had said, his brow furrowed. What he didn't say — and didn't need to say — was that he couldn't stand working for his father anymore.

"Of course." She had almost choked on the words. "Come back and tell me what's really beyond the mountains." If only they had said more. She looked toward the Towers.

"We Zoroastrians revere the earth as sacred," Ābtin had explained when she asked about their purpose. "We do not bury the dead in the ground since that would pollute the earth. Instead we expose the bodies of the dead in the Towers, where birds eat the flesh and clean the bones." Mitrā understood, although the idea of birds eating her dead body still made her shudder. Her family were Muslims and they buried their dead in the ground.

2

Vultures were circling overhead. When Ābtin came back there would be a lot to learn about each other's traditions. Would their families ever allow the marriage she felt so certain about?

She gazed at the Towers, watching the vultures. Was Ābtin still alive, or had he too been fed to the birds? No, she would not think that way. He would come home soon, before she had to give in to her parents who urged her every day to get married.

Just that morning, a man had come to Mitrā's house. The deep resonant sound of the large brass knocker told her a man was at the door. Women used a different knocker with a higher pitch and a sharper sound that faded quickly. Mitrā quickly flung a *chādor* over her head and pulled the edge over her mouth. Even in their own homes, women must cover their hair in the presence of men who are not relatives, though her shawl covered more than that, reaching all the way to the floor.

This man was tall and handsomely dressed in a dark blue coat with colourful embroidery around the hem and collar.

"*Salām khanom,*" he greeted her courteously. "May I speak with Ahmad Moqanni?"

He took her appearance in — what he could imagine under the *chādor* — a tall young woman with proud posture, powerful shoulders and beautiful dark eyes. She wore a red dress with a blue short-sleeved coat over it, mostly covered by the *chādor*. His grey eyes sparkled.

Mitrā looked down modestly, greeted him with "*Salām agha, befarmayid*" and gestured him into the house. He followed her through the vestibule, under the archway leading to the main courtyard, and from there up four big steps to her father's work-room. She and her mother Jeren served the two men tea and cakes, and retired to the kitchen where they could talk.

"He's the coffee seller I told you about," Jeren said, her voice breathless with excitement. "His mother and sister have already come to see me. They are a good family. He is going to propose marriage. Don't look at me like that. True, he's a bit older than you. Don't forget, he's well off and kind. You could do a lot worse."

Mitrā was well aware of this. A successful merchant and the owner of a popular coffee shop, he had a reputation as a gentle man and was well versed in poetry and calligraphy.

"I know I could do worse, Mama. That girl down the street married a man who hardly ever allows her out of the house, even if they go together. Others marry without love." A marriage without love was one thing. Not to marry at all? Unthinkable. How long could she afford to wait for Ābtin?

To avoid conversation with her parents, she left the house and crossed the dry rolling fields to deliver one of the herbal medicines her mother was famous for. The family was Zoroastrian and the patient, a farmer who had broken his arm.

"Please give our profound thanks to your mother," said his wife. "The medicine helps with his pain and the arm is much better."

The woman gave Mitrā a small basket of apples. Mitrā didn't like taking things from people having a hard time but she remembered what her mother had said: "People will give you gifts. We must accept them, even if the people are very poor. They would rather be hungry than ashamed." While some would not have crossed the line between Zoroastrians and Muslims, Jeren believed that healing was for all, even beggars, and certainly for people of different religions. Most families, especially in the rural areas, gathered their own plants but Jeren was often consulted because of her special knowledge.

Mitrā pushed memories of the coffee seller and the farmer aside and took her time on the long walk home from the Towers, enjoying the village where women chatted cheerfully on the street. She liked seeing they hadn't veiled their faces as city women did but was leery about the dogs who came barking and circling around her legs. Nobody had dogs in her neighbourhood. They were considered unclean.

She stopped and bought a scarf of red, gold and a beautiful jewel-like blue. Once she was outside the village she put the scarf on over the top of her *chādor*. What freedom it would be to wear colours in public and uncover her face — to be seen for who she truly was. Then glancing guiltily around, she put the scarf into her pocket.

Once across the barren *sahrā,* she walked through the city, past golden-brown brick houses, neighbourhood mosques and noisy street markets, enjoying the shouts of vendors, the clanging of camel bells and the aroma of horses and spicy foods.

Customers were bargaining, some playful and others intense. The call to prayer sounded from the towering minarets of the Friday Mosque, which shone with diamond-shaped designs and a mixture of blue and turquoise floral and starburst tilework. She went inside to join the prayers and stayed a while after they were over, sitting quietly, enjoying the peace she found there. The atmosphere reminded her of the *sahrā,* the dry grassland where every so often she stopped while harvesting plants with her mother to enjoy the sounds of breezes and birds. Grandeur, simplicity and calm in both places.

As she was leaving the mosque, the Sheikh passed by and nodded to her politely, saying, "*Salām khanom.* And may God be with you."

He was a tall man, with an interesting combination of greying hair and youthful skin. The head cleric and scholar of the city, he was well liked as a community leader and a spiritual one. She returned his polite greeting and continued on her way home.

The alleys were framed by tall mud-brick walls, which provided shade with occasional roofs over the alley to supply structural support. You'd have to be born and raised in Yazd not to get lost there. She passed the vegetable stall where women were gossiping and bargaining, and the small neighbourhood mosque — as short and squat as the Friday Mosque was tall and elegant. Delicious aromas of fresh bread wafted from the open door of the bakery.

At last she arrived home. No one was sitting on the stone bench outside the door, although often in the evening, women might sit there chatting with neighbours, doing needlework and munching sunflower seeds and almonds.

She went under the archway into the main courtyard where a long rectangular pool reflected the blue sky. Mitrā had to keep her *chādor* on in case any visitors were there. At one end, a large, covered area, a *soffeh,* was raised several steps above ground level. Her father often conversed there with potential customers, sitting on cushions.

She continued through another archway into the part of the house reserved for family, through their smaller private courtyard and upstairs to the room she shared with her younger sister, Shirin. They had recently moved upstairs from the cool basement where they slept in the extreme heat of a desert summer.

Shirin's side of the room was littered with papers. She was fascinated by geometry and studied it with their father, Ahmad, at her own insistence. Mitrā could see that her drawings were precise and accurate. Shirin hoped that someday she would be able to help their father with his work, even though she knew full well that engineering was not a womanly pursuit. Still, as long as Ahmad was willing to teach her, she would learn.

Mitrā put away her outer clothing and went in search of their mother, who sat chatting with Shirin in the family courtyard. Jeren smiled and patted the bench beside her.

Later Ahmad returned from his work, gesturing to Mitrā and Jeren. He turned and walked through the main courtyard toward the room he used for keeping his accounts. They followed him into a cozy space with carved wooden decorations around the door and windows, and a well-worn red and blue carpet on the floor.

"Mitrā, that was Hassan the coffee seller who came by today. He has made a good offer for you." He looked her straight in the eye. "I know he is older than you, don't tell me, but he is a good man. We should accept."

Mitrā realized she was lucky her parents allowed her a choice. Not all did. Nor did they all educate their daughters in geometry and herbal medicine and encourage them in their interests. The girls could even read, which was rare for their time and class. Nonetheless.

"Papa." She took a deep breath and spoke firmly. "I am waiting for Ābtin to return."

"Ābtin?" he snapped and began pacing the floor. "That good-for-nothing Zoroastrian carpet weaver's apprentice? Don't think I don't know about your meetings with him. People are talking. It's no good thinking of him, *azizam*. Listen my dear, even his own father has no faith in him. That's why he left town. And where is he now? Could be anywhere, dead or alive! Ābtin won't come back, and if he did, he'd be no match for you. A Muslim girl from a good family? You deserve better. Much better."

"I deserve to follow my heart," Mitrā murmured almost inaudibly. Gritting her teeth, she made herself smile and tease him. "If I'm such a good catch, *bābā*, then why marry me to an older man?"

"*Dokhtar azizam*, you can't wait much longer!" he exploded. "You are already seventeen years old and have refused one good man, the dye maker. How long do you think you can pick and choose before men will stop knocking on your door? Think about your sister. She can't marry before you. Think! And don't take too long about it." He nodded toward the door.

"Yes, *bābā*." She was used to her father's blustering, knowing it was a sign of his love, but this was serious. She took the hint and left the room.

When Mitrā was gone, Ahmad turned to his wife. "Surely she knows that it simply isn't done. Muslim women do not marry

Zoroastrian men. Exasperating girl. Please talk to her about this foolishness. You're the only one she listens to." The whole thing caused an internal conflict he didn't like to think about.

Jeren shook her head. "We both want happiness for our children, to protect them and yet give them freedom."

"Is that even possible? She could be hurt." Besides, how would the family and his business be affected if there were a major scandal?

The next day Mitrā and Shirin went to do errands in the centre of town. Both were covered from head to foot with *chādors*. Underneath hers, Shirin was wearing a new green dress as proudly as if it could be seen. Mitrā was wearing her ordinary blue, although she too held herself well. They presented a contrast as they walked — Mitrā so tall and Shirin so much shorter that sometimes she had to run to keep up.

Shirin took Mitrā's hand. "Let's go this way." Hurrying down a street Mitrā knew was out of the way, they passed shops selling fabrics, clothing and jewellery. Shirin stopped at one selling *ājil*, delicious mixes of nuts and dried fruit. Through the open door, they smelled cinnamon, turmeric and other spices, layered by colour, available in any combination.

Why was Shirin so interested in this particular shop? Mitrā noticed her sister trying not to be obvious as she stared at a young man measuring figs for a customer. He hadn't spotted them. So this was the one Shirin had her eye on. Mitrā had thought there was someone.

"Let's take a look," she said. "We could buy some pistachios to eat on the way home."

Shirin took her arm again and hurried them away. "I don't want him to see me staring."

"Who is he?"

"Just somebody." It was all the reply Mitrā got.

On the way home they passed the *āb anbār*, a huge, covered water cistern that spread over a whole city block. Its dome shone golden in the sun and reached all the way to the ground. Six square towers called *bādgirs* caught the wind and funnelled cool air down over the water to keep it fresh. The girls' house was equipped with two of the wind towers for air conditioning.

They were proud of their father, who had designed the *āb anbār* and overseen its construction. He was a master *moqanni*, a water engineer who designed whole systems. He knew the land in every detail, spending days and weeks out in the *sahrā*, observing, analyzing and storing information in his prodigious memory. He calculated the precise angle the water must take to flow down through the water channels from the rocky mountains to the fields and homes. He designed ways to make the *qanāts* branch off to the homes of the rich before arriving at the huge cisterns where the less wealthy would take their water in large containers. He designed the measuring systems used by those who could afford their own branches of the water system. His son, Mahmood, worked with him, although the younger man didn't have the same enthusiasm or talent for it.

"Look at this!" Shirin stopped to study the steps. "Perfect proportions."

She tried to explain to Mitrā what was so great about it. Her sister clearly wasn't interested. Shirin went on to grumble about their brother, Mahmood, who would inherit the business while having no passion for it.

"It should be me," she said. "Our brother doesn't know a good thing when he sees it."

There were times when all this stopping and calculating irritated Mitrā but today, she was content to wait. This was the place where she'd first met Ābtin.

He had been coming up the Zoroastrian steps as she rounded the corner from the Muslim side. Both stairs led to the same water, so Mitrā had never really understood the point of having two staircases.

That day she wasn't watching where she was going and bumped into him, spilling some of the water from his container. She stepped back, embarrassed.

"*Bebakhshid.* I'm so sorry."

He gave her an enchanting laugh. All he could see were her shining dark eyes and the way she moved, but she felt as if he immediately saw through the *chādor* to her heart within. She was stunned, momentarily speechless.

Perhaps he was not handsome in the way girls usually described young men. He was thin and barely as tall as she was. His face exuded more warmth than beauty. He was wearing a shirt and somewhat dusty baggy pants, both of undyed cotton. Around his waist was a woven belt. Even if he hadn't been on the Zoroastrian steps, his *koshti* belt and clothes would have told her their religions were different.

They stood motionless. Then she pulled herself together and apologized again.

"Spilling a little water doesn't matter at all," he said without taking his eyes off hers. Soon they were sitting in a corner of the square talking. That was probably when the gossip started.

"Isn't that the *moqanni's* daughter?"

"Yes, but who is that man?" Soon the whole town would know. Mitrā and Ābtin paid no attention.

She learned that he was apprenticed to his father, a master carpet weaver with a workshop at home and a small shop in Yazd's main bazaar. She wasted no time finding out exactly where the shop was. After that day she found excuses to visit the carpet shops in the bazaar and saw him again whenever she could — only when his father was not there.

Faraj!

She told Ābtin how she loved gathering plants with her mother and learning about their properties. He spoke of his apprenticeship, his fascination with colours and designs, and his doubts about whether he would ever become a master carpet weaver. His father was so harsh.

"He treats me like a slave," Ābtin said, his voice full of anger and sadness.

It was no surprise when a couple of months later he told her he was going on a journey. To follow his path, find his truth.

What a romantic thing it was to honour that truth, to say, "Let it take as long as it takes." But they were not promised, perhaps never could be, and now he was gone.

How hard it was to wait. Mitrā wanted to forget him, tried to forget him, but his sweetness returned to her again and again. She thought about water — how it flows and finds the gaps, how it cools the flames of yearning.

The two sisters walked on in silence.

Shirin couldn't stay silent for long. She didn't like to see her sister sad. "Let's stop and see Farideh," she said. Their cousin had married early and already had two young children. Through the long afternoons Farideh sat at her loom in the luxurious shade of an immense tree in their courtyard, making beautiful fabrics. Other women gathered to keep her company — and to gossip! That day their friends Maryam and Haideh were there, though some of the regulars were not.

Haideh started off. "Have you heard*? Sara eztevāj mikonad!*"

"Sara? " asked Farideh. "She's not going to marry that *old* man, is she!"

"*Baleh.* She is."

Maryam raised her eyebrows and changed the subject. "Never mind that. I've got news. *Simin va shoharash.*"

11

"What about Simin and her husband?" Shirin asked, glancing around. Simin was not there that day so they could talk about her.

"He wants to take a second wife!"

Mitrā couldn't resist. "Impossible. *Cherā*? Why? They haven't been married so long. She could still give birth to a son. Ah, men!"

Maryam played with her hair, a sly look on her face. "Speaking of men, has anyone seen that new man in town? I think he's handsome."

"You would," said Haideh. "That man is dangerous. Who knows who he is?"

"He says he's from Kermān and that he's a master water engineer. The best in all of Iran."

Farideh spoke again. "How could that be when we already have the best, I ask you? Mitrā and Shirin's father of course. And if that Kermāni is so good, why didn't he stay where he was? He has no relatives here. I think he was in trouble in Kermān and he'll make trouble here. Yesterday he gave me such an indecent look on the street, even though he pretends to be very religious and upright."

"That doesn't mean anything. Lots of pious men leer at women."

The gossip shifted gears. Were all Afghans really sorcerers as some believed? Are our lives ruled by fate or by our family background and personal decisions? The Sheikh had talked about that in a recent sermon. Talk turned to the rights and wrongs of property disputes.

Then Maryam turned to Mitrā.

"Oh Mitrā. When are *you* getting married? Will you marry that coffee merchant? You should! He's so rich. Have you seen his house? Think of the clothes you'll wear and the jewellery. Oh Mitrā, marry the merchant, marry the merchant."

Restless and sick of listening, Mitrā nodded to her sister and left the other women. Even though Shirin loved gossip and would have stayed, she followed without argument. On the way home

Faraj!

Mitrā asked herself whether Ābtin might have found another girl and stayed somewhere with her. And if that were the case, how would she ever know?

2
Jeren
Winter 1662-63

"*Befarmayid*. Please come in." Manizheh ushered Mitrā into a room that was small but comfortable. The last time Mitrā had been here, the woman's son Rostam had been very ill, hovering between life and death. Today Manizheh greeted Mitrā with a big smile and said the boy was considerably better.

Cushions covered in red and gold leaned against the walls and the kitchen took up one corner of the room. Clearly the family was not well off, but there was one exception to the simplicity — a beautiful carpet. Manizheh watched as Mitrā admired the precision of the geometric designs and the harmonious choice of muted blue, green and white.

"My brother-in-law is the carpet weaver Goshtāsp." Mitrā had not heard the name before although she knew a good carpet when she saw one.

"It's very beautiful."

Then the child took her attention. Rostam was about four years old. It was true, his eyes were bright and his colour, better. She gave the woman medicines Jeren had sent.

"My mother will be as happy as I am that he is so much better. Still, try to keep him quiet a little longer and give him these new

14

medicines. Same method as before. Just add hot water and steep them all together. He can take it two or three times a day."

Manizheh offered tea and fruit, looking uncertain as to whether this was the correct thing to do. After all, they both knew that Muslims and Zoroastrians did not eat each other's food, each considering the other's unclean. On the other hand, it would be unthinkably rude not to offer hospitality.

Mitrā accepted. The boy was singing to himself and from time to time his mother spoke to him gently in a language Mitrā did not understand. It must be Dari, she thought, the language spoken by Zoroastrians among themselves. She asked to learn a few words and with a little encouragement the child spoke shyly.

"*Rushkoryak* means hello. If you meet someone in the afternoon." Mitrā tried it out. Rostam laughed. "*Sab bukheir* means good morning."

"That's a lot like Farsi. We say *sob bekheir*. Should be easier than the last one."

Rostam nodded. "And *shav do khash* is good night."

Mitrā left the house a half hour later considerably cheered and took a detour past the Towers of Silence, watching for Ābtin on the road. There was still no sign of him.

When she got home, Jeren was sorting plants in the family courtyard. Some were to be dried, others used fresh and still others made into distillations.

"How is little Rostam? Did the medicine help?"

"He seems to be much better, *khoda ra shokr*."

"Thank God, indeed. We can't prevent trouble from happening. *Inshallah*, let's hope Rostam will recover but there is no refuge from fate." Jeren was always calm, with an inborn serenity. Mitrā wished she could achieve the same within herself.

She wondered about her own fate. Why had she so quickly felt certain she and Ābtin belonged together? Was this destiny or her own imagination, her choice?

They sat together quietly for a while and then Jeren said, "Of all my children, you have the love of the outdoors, the restless spirit of a nomad and a thirst for freedom. That comes with a price. I've never told you the whole story of how your *bābā* and I met. Now that you are thinking about marriage, it's only fair that you know.

"My family is Turkmen and so is my name. Persians sometimes call me Jayrān, probably because the names are similar, but I like to stick with the name I was given at birth. We come from the Qara Qoyunlu tribe as you well know. It's something to be proud of. Our ancestors once ruled much of Iran and brought a lot of books and art here. That's how it is that I taught you and your sister to read.

"We've fallen a long way down since the days when we ruled from Tabriz, our capital. You know that the first Safavid king was the grandson of the last Turkmen king, although that doesn't mean we have any power now. Far from it. The Safavids have been trying to take it away from us for years.

"When I was young, my father was headman of our tribe. We kept sheep in the green mountains north of Mashhad not far from Kalat. It's not like here. There's much more grass, and when you're up in the mountains you can look down and see clouds below. I still miss it.

"Every year we moved at least four times to find grazing for the sheep. Our black tents, dishes, cooking pots, tools, clothes, bedding, everything was loaded up on little desert horses. They're also good on the rugged mountain trails. *Akhal teke,* we call them. We would travel well-worn paths, meeting up with people we knew, hearing news of pastures, water supply, bandits and politics. Our parents cared for their people deeply and well. And they worried about war.

"It's a completely different way of life. As a child I was free. I rode horses and helped my brother with the animals. My older sisters helped our mother and didn't seem to notice my absence. Besides, Turkmen children were always free in the mountains and *sahrā*. I loved the plants and learned about them from my grandmother.

"By the time I turned fifteen, times were harder. Some of our traditional grounds had been taken away. People were being forced to settle, which went against our love of freedom. We were proud, not to be tied to one place. Forced into long detours on our migrations, food got perilously low. We always felt the threat of war from one direction or another. By that time my sisters were married and I was helping my mother with food, sewing and weaving fabrics. Already I missed the mountains and *sahrā*.

"One time we went to the city of Mashhad so my father could try to work things out with the officials. Mother and I went because he felt it was not safe to leave us behind. We took rugs and fabrics to sell in the bazaar.

"Ahmad had come to Mashhad on pilgrimage to the shrine of Imam Reza, the eighth Imam of Shia Islam. They say an Imam is infallible and appointed by God as a leader. Reza was murdered in the place that became the city of Mashhad. The name means martyrdom. That was hundreds of years ago. Your *bābā* came because his mother was ill and he was praying for her recovery. Imam Reza is known as a healer and many go to his shrine for that reason. We Turkmen were Sunni Muslims and knew little about the Shia shrine. We stood astonished, gazing at its glorious golden dome.

"Your *bābā* came into the bazaar later that day looking for a souvenir since everyone who makes the pilgrimage to Mashhad must go home with something. He wanted gifts for his sisters too and bought one of the scarves I had woven the previous winter. Such a handsome man. I hoped to see him again but thought it would never happen.

"That night I heard my parents whispering, thinking I was asleep. They were certainly not talking about Ahmad, the man in the bazaar, although I was still thinking about him.

"'He has made a good offer for her and we need the money,' said my father. This was not the first time I had heard this conversation and it made me shudder.

"My mother said, 'But she's too young. And he's so old. I don't like the look of him. He looks like a cruel man.'

"'Nonsense. How can you tell?'

"'His eyes. I would hate to sell my youngest for money, and to such a man.'

"'Tomorrow I must reply to him.'

"I was wide awake by then. I had seen this man and agreed with my mother — I did not want to marry him! Once my parents were asleep, I got up and dressed in my warmest clothing, took a bit of food and left the caravanserai. After that I never saw my parents or my green mountains again."

Mitrā held her breath.

"It's time to start supper now," said Jeren, getting to her feet.

Reluctantly Mitrā went to the root cellar to bring up carrots and beets. In summer, vegetables were stored over a pool of fresh water instead. And of course, the family of the *moqanni* had a *qanāt* running to their home.

As they prepared the food, she realized her parents would never force her to marry. They couldn't! It was hard to imagine her parents so young and rebellious. She smiled at Jeren, who seemed to understand.

Months passed. It was never the right time to hear the rest of the story as life followed its usual rhythm. In the morning Mitrā went with her neighbour Haideh through narrow alleys to the bakery to buy fresh rounds of nearly flat bread hot from the round oven.

Faraj!

The bread was stuck to the inner walls to bake and came free when it was ready.

In the evening Mitrā loved listening as Ahmad told stories about the great heroes Ali and Hossein, and even about the prophet Mohammad. The family sat around a low table with their legs stretched out toward a container of warm coals under the table. There were love stories and battles — tales of heroes and heroines who wisely faced life's most difficult dilemmas.

After a good story Jeren would recite poetry from memory and then call out, "Sing with me, daughters!" They ate simple meals. Their favourite dish was *ābgusht*, made from lamb on the bone, chickpeas, potatoes, turmeric and onion. Sometimes they ate soup or meatballs with rice and green lentils.

Mitrā watched the roads, waiting for Ābtin, frequently despairing. She knew the roads in every direction now. If you went far enough to the southwest, one of them would lead up into snow-capped mountains, past the town of Taft to Shirāz. From there travellers could connect to the route that took pilgrims to Mecca. The *Hajj* was a journey that every Muslim must make. Ahmad's brother had done it and often reminded Ahmad that he should go too.

Northwest the road led past the Towers of Silence to Esfahān, home of the Shāh. When there wasn't a war, people could travel from there all the way to Constantinople in Turkey. Caravans went north and east to Samarqand, and on to India and China. To the south lay the Persian Gulf.

Once her family had gone east to Māhān beyond the city of Kermān on a much shorter pilgrimage to the mausoleum of the Sufi teacher, Shah Ne'matollah Vali. Just a child at the time, Mitrā remembered climbing the new cupola and gazing out in all directions, wanting to splash in the fountain and run through the garden. That was not allowed!

19

Holidays came and went. Ramadan, the month of fasting, passed. Ahmad observed it but Jeren often made exceptions for herself and the children. The lights of Yaldā shone at the winter solstice and everyone ate pomegranates, which bring the power of many joining together. The red fruit also represented life and good health.

Mitrā did not marry the coffee merchant. He had lost patience, retracted his offer and married another girl. Shirin had been promised to the man from the fruit and nut shop who was a distant cousin named Ali. They wanted to marry but she had to wait for her older sister, which added to the pressure. Silence fell over the household.

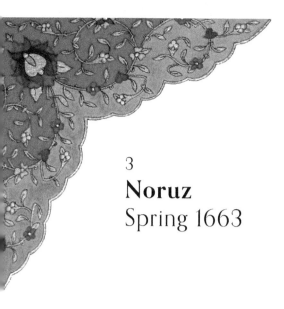

3
Noruz
Spring 1663

At the beginning of spring, Mitrā's family always had a party for the Noruz holiday. They invited their large family and included Ahmad's colleagues and customers, their neighbours and some of the town's notables. By long-standing family custom, one or two strangers were always invited.

"You never know what form God will take when he comes to the door," Jeren repeated every year.

As she dressed for the evening, Mitrā considered the layering of her clothes. Under her dress she wore wide leggings with embroidered cuffs that came down over her leather slippers. This year she had a new dress in dusty-rose pink with floral designs. Two-layered dresses were fashionable. The pink bodice was tight and low-cut while the skirt was wide and had a slit up the front. Underneath the dress was a long red shirt that showed at the neckline and down the front. She wore a wide black sash, a gold cap and jewellery, and her carefully braided hair glittered with colourful ornaments.

As Mitrā dressed, she thought of her other layers: daughter, sister, friend. With any luck she would become an herbalist and a good wife. Private lives, public lives, expectations, truth. She looked in the mirror and for the first time realized that she was a woman, no longer a girl.

Music filled the air. Servants who had been hired for the occasion hurried from kitchen to courtyard. Guests were eating and chatting, enjoying the warm weather. The men gathered in the main courtyard and the women, in the family courtyard. Jeren was hosting the women and stood out in a dramatic dress of blue-green with a sash adorned with classic Turkmen embroidery — strong trees and a bright sun.

On her way to the staircase leading to the family courtyard, Mitrā stopped by a small window overlooking the men's party. Even though a woman wasn't supposed to show herself unveiled where she could be seen by men who were not relatives, it seemed safe enough — just for a moment. Who was going to be looking anyway? The men would be busy with food and talk.

Many of the men were familiar. Her cousins and uncles were there, also Bābak, a much beloved friend of the family. Who was to know that he was a long-term employee of Ahmad's and not a relative? Besides, he knew almost as much about water systems as her father did and deserved respect.

Some men she didn't recognize but, from the style of their clothing with its silver and gold embroidery, it was obvious that they were important. One even wore a robe made of *termeh*, a very expensive fabric made of silk for which Yazd was famous. He might be the mayor or a judge.

Among them was a stranger. The other men did not greet him with the easy familiarity of long acquaintance and a few kept a significant distance from him without being obviously rude. The stranger's clothes were unusual — an elaborate turban and a short robe over tight pants. They looked costly but were carelessly worn. His sharp nose stood out on his narrow, lined face. Mitrā thought he looked mean, shifty.

Could this be the man that her friends had gossiped about? If so, inviting him to the party had been a bold move on her father's part. Ahmad had laughed about it over supper a few days before.

"Bābak tells me he's come here from the city of Kermān to compete with me as a water engineer. Am I supposed to consider that a great honour? He has met the man and can invite him to the party. I'll get a good look at him. Then of course he'll owe me."

"I've heard he frequents the most conservative mosque in town," Jeren added. "Probably for the sake of his reputation. He's even trying to ingratiate himself with the Sheikh."

One glance from her window and Mitrā decided religion was the furthest thing from his mind.

When she arrived, his eyes had been moving rapidly over the crowd. Now he glanced up and focused in her direction. It was unnerving. He looked as if he had recognized her, or perhaps seen a ghost. She dodged away from the window and continued on her way down the stairs with only one glance back. He was still looking up although she had disappeared from his line of sight.

Evil seemed to surround him while at the same time there was something fascinating about him. Surely some women would fall for him, like the gossipy Maryam. In spite of the heat, Mitrā shivered, as if she had seen the angel of death.

Mitrā entered the courtyard, still shaken, and moved among the women. "*Salām*, Auntie Golnaz. *Salām*, Haideh." She began to relax while greeting cousins, aunts and neighbours, and joined Shirin serving plates of sweets, fruit and nuts. There was *pashmak*, fluffy as cotton candy, *qotābha* dumplings, sweet *bāqlava* and *sharbat*. Real Yazd treats.

The stranger retreated from her thoughts.

A few days later she saw him again while in the bazaar with her mother and sister. Again he tried to catch her eye. She kept her glance modestly on the ground and turned away, trying to be invisible. If only she weren't so tall.

Two days later Mitrā's father received a visit from the man, who indeed claimed to be the water engineer from Kermān.

"My name is Nāder," he said. "As you probably know I am newly arrived in your city. I would like to take your elder daughter as my second wife." He lowered his voice and mentioned a generous financial offer.

Ahmad was outraged at the insult. After accepting his hospitality? And with no *ta'arof*, no polite talk to lead into his request?

"My daughter will marry as first wife or not at all," he replied firmly. At least this year, he thought. If she finally gives up on the absent carpet weaver's apprentice. What could the man's motivation be? To demean his competitor's reputation by insulting his daughter? Now the man was sneering. His voice, unpleasantly nasal.

"Tell me, *agha* Ahmad, do you really think you can do better for a daughter who roams the barren lands and has been seen doing strange things with plants? A girl who has been seen unveiled and has twice refused to marry? Hah!"

Ahmad showed him to the door with very cold courtesy. True, he'd have a few choice words with his daughter about keeping her veil in place although he seriously doubted the truth of that accusation. She knew better. He would defend her against slander in any way he could.

Mitrā saw the Kermāni again on the road a few days later when she and her mother were out collecting plants. As his horse pawed the ground, the man's shifty eyes squinted from behind the heavy woven shawl that protected his face from the blowing sand. He was gazing into one of the valleys with a water channel running through it. A row of openings called *chāh*, or well, showed where the men went down to clean and maintain the *qanāt*. Even now there was equipment beside one of them. Someone must be there, working underground. Maybe it was her brother, Mahmood.

The Kermāni must have heard their horse. He glanced at the two women and then rode off at a gallop, down the hill, across the valley and up the other side.

Mother and daughter rode a fine horse, one of the family treasures bought in honour of Jeren. Nomads valued horses almost above all else and Jeren was known as an expert horsewoman who could outride just about anyone in Yazd.

When he was out of sight, they tossed their veils back and turned their attention to the plants. Jeren quizzed her daughter about the various flowers, roots and leaves. Mitrā knew most of them.

"This is henna and there is some camomile over there. Is this one frankincense?"

"Yes it is, and over on the other side of the valley we'll find astralagus and mallow. We may find one you haven't seen yet too. It's got leaves like a fern and is good for treating shock. It's called *siāvshun*. And of course you know *shātereh* — we use it for smudging the house."

"The *sahrā* seems totally bare until you look closer. It's so rich!"

Jeren went on to talk about which parts of the plant to take, whether it was best to do it now or wait until later in the season, whether to dry or boil it, and what it was good for. Mitrā was kept busy trying to remember it all.

Jeren seemed to be able to communicate with the plants directly, speaking to them in her childhood language and then cocking her head to one side, listening for their replies.

"I'm having a conversation with the soul of creation," she said, smiling at her daughter.

Mitrā listened carefully. She enjoyed being outside the city, feeling the freshness of the breeze, hearing the birds calling overhead. Mountains loomed in the distance, beyond the vast treeless expanse.

"The other day I was in the Friday Mosque," Mitrā said. "There was such a peaceful feeling under the great dome. The same feeling I get out here. How can two places that are so different create the same sensation?"

"Could it be that the peaceful feeling is in you?" Jeren laughed and went on working.

Mitrā wondered what it would be like underground but had never asked anyone, not even her father. Could someone actually walk from one place to another or would there be too much water? It was odd for the daughter of a *moqanni* not to know the answer but she had always had a terror of being underground and didn't like to admit it. Was it claustrophobia, the ever-present danger of the earth collapsing or just being enclosed in darkness? She couldn't say and didn't know where the fear came from. Her sister did not share it.

Jeren saw Mitrā's faraway expression and wanted to cheer her up with a laugh. "I've heard stories of thieves hiding in *qanāts*. Sometimes they hire rogue *moqannis* to build underground hideouts for their stolen goods. Your father once heard a tale about a tunnel that crossed under an international boundary. That was a long way from Yazd though."

Mitrā shook off her gloomy thoughts. "Stories do get bigger as they travel. Maybe those crooks even took horses through the tunnel or better yet, elephants."

They worked, digging roots, piling plants up, placing them in baskets, moving from one spot to another. Several months had passed since Jeren told her story of leaving the mountains. Now Mitrā wanted to hear the rest. The time seemed right.

"What happened after you left your family?"

Jeren took time finding a comfortable hollow to sit in.

"Once I got outside the caravanserai, I had no idea where to go and just started walking, with no plan, knowing only that I would not marry a cruel old man, even to help support my family. I left while my parents were sleeping and walked through the night, ending up outside the shrine of Imam Reza just as the stars were fading and the gentle light of dawn was growing brighter.

"You may not believe this but I met your father beside the well outside the shrine. He had just finished washing before going in to pray and recognized me from the market where he had bought one of my scarves. He saw my distress and invited me to sit down at the base of the well. I would never have imagined telling something so personal to a complete stranger — a man at that. It all came out. Fear and anger at my father's betrayal. My yearning for the mountains.

"'Come with me,' he said. 'Don't worry, I won't harm you or dishonour you. I'm leaving Mashhad today. We'll figure something out.'

"Later he told me that at the time he had no idea what we could possibly figure out or what his parents would say. He just knew he wanted to help me. It felt like a necessary part of his pilgrimage. Somehow to him, an act of kindness would activate the blessings he had received from Imam Reza and help his mother recover. It would always remind him to be generous to others. After having run from an unknown man, I trusted Ahmad and was willing to put my fate in his hands. He loaned me men's clothes so that we could travel together without problems.

"We spent long days crossing the desert and *sahrā* on the way back, keeping an eye out for bandits. I'll always remember seeing the saffron fields when the purple flowers were blooming — huge fields of them. It felt so good to see the first tree as we approached the oasis city of Tabas after weeks of travel."

Mitrā knew this part of the story well — it was a kind of proverb in their family. Whenever the first ray of light appeared in a seemingly unsolvable problem Jeren would say, "There's the first tree."

As Jeren finished her story, Mitrā smiled. "Thanks for telling me."

They continued working in silence and later separated, staying just within sight of each other on opposite sides of the row of wells. After an hour or so Mitrā thought she saw the Kermāni again, galloping back the way he had come.

Suddenly there was a rumbling noise, an uneasiness in the earth and a muffled shout from underground. Both women stood up, scanning the horizon. Their eyes met over the distance. Could it be an earthquake? Everything seemed still. No, something was different. There was an indentation in the row of wells, the one where the equipment was.

Mitrā ran, calling, "Who is there? Are you injured? Speak to me. Is it you, Mahmood?"

A muffled voice answered, clearly in pain. "I'm here. Bābak. Don't try to get down here. It's too dangerous."

Bābak, of course. Bābak was like an uncle to Mitrā and he treated her as if she were his own daughter. She in turn always called him *amu*, uncle. She had known him all her life.

She came closer. "*Amu* Bābak, are you injured? Can you breathe?"

Jeren arrived. "Move back, Mitrā! The earth could give way."

Mitrā moved back a few steps. "*Amu* Bābak is trapped down there. Please go and fetch help. I'll stay here."

Jeren hated to leave her daughter alone but this was the time for speed and she would go faster alone. The nomad horsewoman was on her way in an instant, calling out, "Stay here! Talk to him but don't go any closer!"

As soon as she was out of sight, Mitrā went closer and began moving rocks. Gently, carefully. The *chāh* opened before her.

Pulleys had fallen in. The ladder was partly broken but still looked navigable.

It was very dark down there. As her eyes adjusted, she saw *Amu* Bābak bent over inside the channel. Something heavy was lying across his long legs, which were half-submersed in water. His usually cheerful face was pinched with pain. She picked her way toward him.

"Go back," he whispered.

"Mother's gone for help," she said and then gingerly tried to lift the heavy ceramic object that lay across his legs. In most places, the soil was compact enough to hold the shape of the channel. But in some cases, the earth was too soft and a ceramic ring would be installed to hold the shape. Here, part of the support ring had fallen. It was heavy, awkwardly curved and hard to get a grip on but, with adrenalin fuelling her strength, Mitrā lifted it momentarily from his legs. Straining, Bābak pulled himself out from under it — just before she lost her hold and the ceramic piece dropped back onto the ground.

Water was rising. The channel was blocked with rubble below the well. Resting his arm across her shoulder, she helped him out from under the damaged support to the side of the channel. They sat down as far as possible from the water, underneath the opening where the air was fresher. She used her scarf to stop his bleeding. More rubble fell, closer to them.

They waited as the water continued to rise. Bābak tried to move. Standing was too painful and getting up the ladder without more help would be impossible. The water rose higher. It seemed as if they had been there forever.

"Go, Mitrā," he said quietly, but she stayed and sang songs remembered from childhood. Before long he joined her until at last they heard horses' hooves and a shout.

"This is the spot!" It was Jeren.

Faces appeared from above — Mitrā's father Ahmad, her brother Mahmood and others. After a flurry of activity and a near miss when the ladder broke, at last they were out and dried off. Jeren immobilized Bābak's legs.

Mitrā breathed a sigh of relief. Only now did it occur to her that she'd done the very thing she was most afraid of. She'd gone underground and stayed without fear, all because she was focused on Bābak.

Finally they got home and took Bābak into one of the guest rooms. Jeren gave them both *siāvshun* tea for their shock and continued to nurse Bābak. Soon his wife arrived and sat with him, bringing her own medicines to complement Jeren's.

Bābak and his wife returned to their own home the next day.

There was much debate around town about what could have caused the collapse. The *qanāt* was well built and not very old, that much was certain. Why would the fired-clay support ring give out? Bābak recalled noticing substantial cracks in the ring but, by the time he decided to get out, it was too late.

The next day Ahmad rode out with Mahmood to examine the place thoroughly. When he got home to his waiting family, he took off his muddy boots and said, grim-faced, "The support that fell on Bābak appears to have been deliberately cut. It was not worn out or corroded by water."

"Once the damage was done, would a horseman crossing the line of wells be enough to trigger a collapse?" Mitrā asked. "I saw the man from Kermān galloping over the *qanāt*. The timing was right but who could his target have been?"

Ahmad sighed. "It could it have been me or for that matter any of my workmen, to call my engineering into question." He thought it best not to mention that it could have been because he had refused to let him marry Mitrā.

"That's terrible! He could have killed someone, anyone. Or doesn't he care about that?"

Her father sighed again. "Maybe not. But we have no proof about any of it."

Gossip started spreading about Mitrā.

"What was she doing underground with a man she's not related to?" Maryam asked, and for once Simin agreed with her.

"What was she doing underground at all? Plus I heard she took off her scarf to stop his bleeding. Of course it was good to help him but I don't want her as my friend anymore."

Her parents supported her staunchly. Bābak's wife insisted Mitrā was to be admired for having saved a man's life. Mitrā's best friend Haideh agreed, saying pointedly that Mitrā had done what any courageous woman would do. But others, like Simin and Maryam, shunned her.

Worst of all was Nāder Kermāni. He went to the Sheikh and accused Mitrā outright of sorcery. "I have seen her making pagan rituals over that very place," he said.

The Sheikh couldn't see why she would do such a thing, especially around her father's *qanāt*. He'd need to find out more about this stranger. He'd never heard a bad word about Mitrā although he'd keep his ears open about her too. He'd always advised people to consider the source of their information before making accusations. "Who is telling you?" he would ask and now he decided to take his own advice.

"The *moqanni's* family is of course very familiar with the *sahrā*," he said. "Don't accuse others unless you are very certain you have good evidence." He made it clear the interview with Nāder Kermāni was over.

Still, the gossip got around. Whose word would be believed?

I've been waiting a whole year for Ābtin, Mitrā thought, and now I'm waiting for public opinion to decide my fate. She felt she'd been picked up by a whirlwind and dumped back down as a different person.

The water system was repaired and eventually the gossip died down as other subjects replaced it. For Mitrā though, the taint remained. Would Ābtin never come back? And if he did, would he still love her?

One very hot day Mitrā returned to the Towers of Silence. How innocent she had been when she'd first stood there a year ago. How things had changed. The sun beat down relentlessly and dust rose from the road with the slightest breeze. For the first time she felt completely discouraged.

She turned to go when she heard something. Singing, coming from the mountains — or was it even closer? Could it be? She didn't want to get too excited but her heart was beating faster. It was worth singing back.

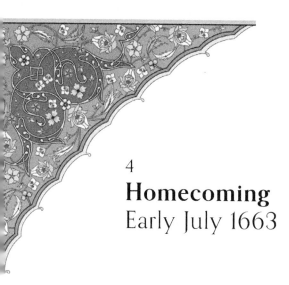

4
Homecoming
Early July 1663

Ābtin sped up when he saw the tall woman before him. She had lifted the hem of her *chādor* and was running across the *sahrā*, getting closer but taking forever to come into focus in the shimmering heat. He ran. The veil fell from her face, revealing rosy cheeks. At last he was certain. The two stopped an arm's length away from each other and stood motionless, wanting to embrace. This was the first time he had ever seen her unveiled and it left him speechless. After what felt like an eternity, they both smiled and then laughed.

Mitrā pulled her *chādor* up over her hair as they walked toward the city. After a while, they sat down in the shade of the Towers. There was so much to talk about but where to begin?

"I knew you'd come," she said, despite her recent despair.

"I knew you'd be here," he replied, in spite of all he had feared.

The whole past year began pouring out: Mitrā's feeling the earth shake when the *qanāt* collapsed, Ābtin's sense of being buried alive during a sandstorm, her troubles with the man from Kermān, his friendship with some fishermen at the Caspian Sea, the day Mitrā saw the connection between the peace within the mosque and that of the *sahrā*, a carpet seller who read poetry to

Ābtin, her singing to a man caught in the *qanāt* collapse, his time with a wise old woman and her plants.

They came to the village and walked in silence toward the gate in the high wall that surrounded his home. This was the village where she had brought medicines to the child Rostam. There were about twenty mud-brick houses, most with barns behind them, a communal *āb anbār* for their water supply, a bath house, a fire temple and beyond that nothing but the *sahrā* in three directions. The grand expanse of azure sky was always with them. To the north they could see the minarets of Yazd.

Until now Mitrā had not known exactly where Ābtin lived. From the sound of things, there were chickens in the yard. She had known their families were different but seeing the place brought it home in a new way.

Thump! The gate crashed open and a shaggy brown dog nosed his way out. The dog did his best to bark at Mitrā and at the same time leap joyfully on Ābtin, who couldn't help laughing. Mitrā backed off, terrified.

"Don't worry. He's friendly. He just doesn't know you. Shhhh, Rafiq."

She was not convinced. Everyone she knew said dogs were unclean and vicious besides. Except her mother, who seemed to ignore them as they did her. The dog now had two paws on Ābtin's shoulders and was licking his face — tail wagging, ears flapping. Mitrā squirmed.

"How can dogs tell a Muslim from a Zoroastrian?" she asked, positive that it was true.

"I doubt they know much about religion. I do know that they can tell a person who will treat them kindly from one who will kick them, which I don't think you would do. Show him your hand."

That was even scarier but she tried.

A voice came from inside. "Who's there? Rafiq, come here!" Ābtin took Mitrā's arm and pulled her down the street.

"That's my little sister Katayun. I'm not ready to go in quite yet," he said. "I'll walk you to the edge of the city — in case you meet any more dogs."

They crossed fields green with young plants and others that were bone dry. At last they came to the first houses of Yazd. After all this time apart, it was hard to say goodbye but soon it would be getting dark. Her parents would worry.

Ābtin hesitated. "How can I go in? I'm a different person than when I left."

"Go. They'll be so happy to see you."

"Maybe. The thing is that I'm not the same person as before. I'm an artist now. Never a slave again." Would it be so, back in his old environment? Or would habits of submission and anger take over?

"Ābtin, trust yourself."

How different it was, Mitrā realized, to have parents who trusted her. Then again, what did she really know of his family? She'd only heard about his father. She hadn't even heard his sisters' names until now and she knew nothing about his mother. Besides, she too had grown. She was a healer now and a woman who had refused to marry. Everything had changed — except her certainty about Ābtin.

"Go back. They are waiting. Meet me tomorrow at the *āb anbār*." She mentioned the water cistern without thinking. The first place they had met seemed like a good place to start again.

Then she was gone.

He stood a while longer, recalling a day shortly before he'd left on his journey.

Spring 1662

Ābtin had been sorting wool samples from his father's racks, trying out combinations of colour for a carpet design he'd been imagining. It was a question of subtleties. Not just any blue, not just any red. Then his father appeared.

"You lazy good for nothing, get back to work. What are you doing? What's this mess? Put these things away and in the right places. Stupid boy, can't tell a camel from a cow. Get back to the job I gave you! Those skeins don't wind themselves you know."

"Father, how can I learn if I never do any work of my own?" He was angry. Again.

He'd asked before and knew it was pointless. His father, Goshtāsp, was a master carpet weaver with a good business but definitely no interest in his son's dreams — the patterns, the maps he saw with his inner eye. Nor was he interested in teaching the skills of colour selection and carpet design.

Ābtin worked hard in the shop doing routine tasks. He swept the floors, served tea to customers, set up looms, measured paper and made the grids that Goshtāsp used for drawing his final carpet patterns to scale. In the evenings he practised repetitive weaving motifs. He was permitted to weave belts with just one repeating pattern, usually the cypress tree. Good of course but not inspiring since it was the only thing he was allowed to do. Ābtin knew in his soul that he'd never really see the details until he understood the whole. It was just the way his mind worked. He itched to draw his own designs to scale and knot them from a large plan.

Goshtāsp's attitude didn't make sense. Surely one day Ābtin would inherit the business and then he would have to do everything. He'd overheard some people in the bazaar say that his father was more technically brilliant than inspired. So maybe he just couldn't see that his son's mind worked differently. That didn't make sense either. It made him mad.

That evening his father had leaned over his shoulder and said, "Keep working on that cypress motif until you get it right. After that, do it backwards." Then with a sly look he added, "Don't even think of marrying until you've mastered your craft." As if he knew about Mitrā.

Who could have seen them together? Someone from the village who happened to be in town? Or that nosy old man with the shop next to theirs in the bazaar? Ābtin had paced up and down the road, trying to calm down, determined to find a caravan and go on a journey. Although Yazd was always dry in summer, this year was worse. A real water shortage was predicted and he could see signs of it as he walked. Plants were turning brown sooner than usual, creeks drying up, dogs panting. Good reason to go now, Ābtin thought. One less person needing water in the house.

A few days after the conversation with his father, he found a caravan master and told him he'd like to sign on. The *kārvān sālār* looked Ābtin up and down.

"Are you prepared to work?" he asked.

"Certainly."

"Well, you're in luck. The guy who was supposed to show up changed his mind. Come back tomorrow. You'll help with the animals when we stop and do whatever else I give you to do. For that, you'll get food when we have any. Agreed?"

The next day while everyone was busy, Ābtin crept out of the house carrying a small bag with extra clothes, a bit of food and a small portable loom. He'd taken it apart and tied the pieces to his backpack. He'd told his father some time before that he wanted to go away to Esfahān for a month. Goshtāsp had snorted, not believing his son would go anywhere. Hardly believing it himself, Ābtin walked to the caravanserai.

In the hot weather, they travelled by night. There was plenty of noise as the camel drivers loaded up bales of Yazdi fabrics destined for Esfahān. Camel bells clanged and Ābtin heard at least three languages he didn't understand. He spoke Farsi of course and also Dari, the language Zoroastrians spoke among themselves. That was all.

He had only told two people that he was going — Mitrā and his sister Rudābeh, who was sworn to secrecy.

July 1663

That was so long ago now. A whole year of a very different life. Ābtin walked through the gate and slowly crossed the courtyard. The house was directly in front of him. Smoke rose from the kitchen fire. Chickens scratched in the yard.

The carpet workshop was behind the house, out of sight in the growing darkness although it probably looked exactly the same as always. Double doors led to the open space inside where looms of several sizes held projects in the works.

The family home was on the edge of the village farthest from the city — he could smell the pungent *sahrā* grasses on the breeze. A profound silence was broken only by the occasional mooing of their cow. Familiar aromas of the family cow and a whiff of his mother's famous soup with dumplings made him feel he'd never left home.

Ābtin stood a little longer in silence until he heard the dog's tail beating on the closed door. He took a deep breath and went in. Rafiq leapt up on him again, eagerly wagging his tail. Four faces turned at once — Goshtāsp, his mother Sindokht, and younger sisters Rudābeh and Katayun. He could hardly recognize Rudābeh, sixteen by now. She had become a young woman while he was gone, while at fourteen Katayun looked almost the same. There was a moment of disbelieving silence followed by hugs and tears. Even his father looked relieved.

"So there you are. It's about time," he muttered gruffly.

Silence returned. Sindokht covered it by going to the kitchen to fry bread laced with onions and turmeric to go with the soup. "You must be starving. You look so thin." She and the girls got to work. This only made things worse.

"Where have you been?" Goshtāsp grumbled when they were alone. "You said it would be a month. You never even told me you were really going. Disobedient lout. Where are the dyes you said you'd bring back? ... Why?"

Ābtin sighed. "Father, I made my living for a year by weaving." He'd forgotten about the dyes. "I've been to the shores of the Caspian Sea."

Always an imposing man, tall with a look of authority, Goshtāsp now made the most of it by standing up and moving a few steps closer. Ābtin noticed that his father's beard had streaks of grey. A chill went down his back yet surprisingly he was not afraid.

"Did you ever once think of your mother?" Goshtāsp was nearly shouting now. "She was worried sick."

Mother's voice rose from the kitchen. "Don't start, *azizam*. Just be grateful he's back."

"I needed you in the shop."

Ābtin had no answer. He felt familiar prickles of old anger. Didn't the man even want to know where his son had been and what he had seen and done?

As always Sindokht fed the dog before the people. There was a spate of talk — so much had happened in Yazd during the past year. The water shortage ended with a little more rainfall than usual, most of it in the mountains. There had even been some snow melt, the runoff carefully gathered into the water systems. There had been marriages, deaths and births. One of the *qanāts* had collapsed and a Muslim girl saved a man trapped inside.

"It was Bābak. Do you remember him?" Sindokht asked. "My sister's brother-in-law. He's fine now — just walks with a bit of a limp. That Muslim girl's mother is the one who makes medicines. They both helped him."

No one in their community knew what to think of the girl who saved Bābak.

"Not modest although she is brave," said Rudābeh.

Sindokht added, "A strange girl. She refused to marry a rich coffee merchant as well as a dye-maker."

"She is the *moqanni's* daughter," said Katayun.

Ābtin blushed. Could this be Mitrā? She'd spoken about a *qanāt* collapse but had said nothing about rescuing anybody. She'd never mentioned that her father was the water engineer. Would Mitrā really have refused a good marriage offer? His heart beat faster.

"You know we're starting on pilgrimage?" asked Sindokht. "To Pir Bānu-Pārs. We'll celebrate your homecoming. We leave first thing in the morning, day after tomorrow. It'll be the perfect chance to clean you up from all that travel contamination."

He wouldn't tell his mother, at least not right away, about everything he had eaten and the people from various religions and nations he had met. It was hard to consider that contamination when most of the time he felt so blessed by the connections he'd made.

Of course he would go with them, from one kind of pilgrimage to another. Pir Bānu-Pārs was a shrine located two days' journey from their village in the mountains north of Yazd. They made the trip every year at the beginning of July.

Ābtin gave his family the gifts he had made. For Katayun there was a wide belt in sea blue and green. She was the baby of the family and would be getting ready for her initiation. For Rudābeh he had made a belt recalling the desert in red and yellow. He knew she loved the *sahrā* as she loved their own garden. He'd made a bag for his mother with blue and white to represent the sacred mountain Damāvand. Most difficult of all was the bag for his father in shades of green that reminded him of the carpet of trees at the mountaintop. He used the cypress motif, honed to perfection and with many variations. Goshtāsp turned the bag inside out and counted knots. He nodded almost imperceptibly.

That night Ābtin climbed the ladder to his old place, a corner of the house that seemed to have been an afterthought to the second floor. The little room was still his, pretty much as he'd left it a year before. Cool air came through the window and the full moon shone over the *sahrā*. His sisters were giggling from the room next to his.

When Mitrā got home she went straight to the cool basement. Jeren gave her a curious look. "What happened?"

Mitrā had debated whether to tell her mother right away or not and now she couldn't resist. "He's back! Oh Mama, he's back!"

Jeren hesitated only for a moment and then took her in her arms. "I am so happy for you. Surely the desert woman must have helped him." Desert woman, helper of the lost and desperate. Mitrā had heard tales of her helping people find water — those who were kind and truly seeking. Desert woman lived inside a sacred mountain and came out to provide whatever was needed. Then she would disappear again. People made offerings to her while travelling. Mother had embroidered the desert woman's symbol on her shawl to protect them when they left the house.

Mitrā chattered on about how much taller Ābtin had grown and the wisdom that shone from his eyes. Jeren smiled. Later she said, "My dear daughter, I hate to say this. You must know it won't be easy to be his friend. And you certainly can't marry him. He has a different religion and beliefs, and comes from a different background."

Unwillingly Mitrā thought of how she had shuddered as she watched vultures swooping over the Towers of Silence. Her mother was speaking from experience. After all, marriage between a Sunni Turkmen nomad and an urban Shia Persian could not have been easy, even without the vultures. There were both religious and political differences.

As children, she and her siblings had only heard the romantic story of their mother meeting the handsome *moqanni* while he was on pilgrimage and that she had returned with him to Yazd. They had never known exactly how their parents met — only that they had married for love. The rest had been a secret until that day in mid-winter when Jeren had begun to confide in her. Now Mitrā wondered how her father's family had responded. It must have been a shock to see their son come home from pilgrimage with a young woman from the north. They now loved her as their own but what had it been like at first?

The next day Mitrā and Ābtin met at the *āb anbār* and sat down nearby. They gazed up at the water cistern's great dome and then into each other's eyes.

"Did you really save a man's life when the *qanāt* collapsed?"

"Well, after all it was my *Amu* Bābak. I had to do something. People exaggerate though. I was singing so I didn't notice the time go by. Who knows if I saved him?" Mitrā blushed. She too was exaggerating. The experience had been terrifying in retrospect and she still shuddered at the thought of being underground. It had seemed like a century before help came.

"You stayed there underground? You're brave. And did you really refuse to marry a rich coffee merchant?" Now he realized that her *Amu* Bābak was the same as his. Not a true uncle to either one — it was simply an affectionate name.

Mitrā laughed, embarrassed. "How do you know these things? Oh well, everybody knows. Tell me what it was like beyond the mountains."

He decided it was wiser to leave the coffee merchant out of the conversation for now and began his story.

42

5

Ābtin

"There were good times and bad times on that trip. The caravan I hired on with was headed for Esfahān and beyond. At some stops, other travellers would join us. Some had their own donkeys or camels while others would rent the animals from the caravan master. There were a lot of camel drivers and guards to protect us and the cargo.

I was lucky to be with them — the road is dangerous. There were tales of lions and tigers, not to mention bandits, but our guards were strong and well-trained. We knew they could deal with anything. There were also men who knew where every well could be found, even during a water shortage. Of course on the rare occasion we came to an oasis, it felt like heaven.

"At first the road was familiar since I'd been as far as Ardakān when we went on pilgrimage. Soon our caravan continued beyond where I'd ever been, crossing rocky mountains and then real desert. Day after day, the camel bells clanged as the men sang and laughed. Sometimes I got to ride a camel but mostly I walked. They had taken me on to work around the camp when we stopped to rest, which was mainly during the middle of the day since it was so hot.

"Day after day, the sun shone in a clear blue sky. Night after night, we travelled under a carpet of stars. Most of the time, the camels behaved well but other times they were so stubborn! They'd stop and refuse to move. When a young one ran away, I had to chase him.

"One day as we moved along the swirling sands, the caravan master shouted right out of nowhere, 'Take shelter!' The camel drivers obeyed him at once. They circled the camels up and took the loads down from their backs, using the loads to make shelter for us. It was late afternoon and we had just started out after the mid-day rest so it seemed an odd time to stop.

"Then we saw what the caravan master had seen. A huge cloud of sand — the size of a small mountain — was rushing our way. We hunkered down and covered ourselves as best we could with scarves and coats. In a sandstorm, you've got to to cover every opening into the body — eyes, ears, nose, mouth."

Mitrā nodded. She'd heard about sandstorms.

"We waited. The storm struck full force. Winds howled for hours and, no matter how well we'd bundled up, sand got in everywhere.

"At last the winds died down and little by little we dug ourselves out. At first I couldn't move and that was scary. But at least I wasn't alone with an injured man the way you were. Finally I got up and looked around. The guys were laughing at me but I didn't care.

"The landscape had changed so much that we couldn't recognize where we were. Luckily our caravan master had an uncanny sense of direction. He just took his bearings — I don't know how — and pointed us in the right direction. You know some caravans have a special guide with them if the roads are hard to follow. But our *kārvān sālār* was our guide as well.

"That was not the only thing I liked about the caravan master. In the evening he would give me a job to do. 'Hey Yazdi, get the fire going but first of all get that rogue camel back here!' Things like that. When I did well, he would say, 'Good work, Ābtin. *Āfarin*, Yazdi!' He was not like my father at all.

"On we went. I had brought along a small portable loom and some wool, planning to weave a few small things — belts and maybe a saddlebag or two — and sell them in the towns to make some money. As time went by though, my interest in the weaving grew. I made things from my own ideas instead of always following instructions. Could I somehow capture that bird just as it took off? Or match the colour of the rocks in the early evening as the sun went down?

"Our camel drivers came from all over — Iran, Afghanistan, Azerbaijan. One was even from India, and there was a guy from way beyond Samarqand who stopped at every spring and mountain pass to make offerings — a little food or tobacco, a small coin. Sometimes, he simply placed one stone on top of another.

'Everything in the world has a spirit,' he told me, 'even the rocks. These offerings let the spirits of the place know we mean well.'

"Most of the men would stop to pray, sometimes all at the same time, sometimes at different times. Nobody fussed about food rules. The only time I tried to hide my religion was when a mulla joined the caravan — you can never tell what they'll do. Certainly he would have given us all a stern talking-to about eating together, which would have been uncomfortable for me and some of the others for that matter. Luckily he didn't stay with us for long. Either he didn't notice or else he just kept quiet about it.

"A few weeks later we finally came to the city of Esfahān and stopped at a caravanserai. It was a lot like the ones here — a square building made of bricks with a courtyard in the middle. The bricks were the same mixture of clay, sand and hay that we use in our house. The caravan master was hoping to get fresh animals there and fill the water bags. Some travellers left our caravan and others would join when it moved on. I think they were headed to Baghdad or even farther. I really wanted to go straight north and figured I'd be one of those who left the caravan.

"Many travellers were already there, pitching camps, setting up their wares under the building's arches. The best places faced the internal courtyard and were all taken. Our caravan master found a spot on the outside. There I sold the first of my saddlebags and my spirits rose. I wandered around, drinking in the sights. There were men repairing shoes, saddles and pots, and people selling rice, nuts and tea. Best of all was having a delicious hot meal. Using money from selling the bag, I treated my new friends to lamb kebabs and rice with a cup of wine."

Ābtin stopped and looked at Mitrā. "By the way, please don't tell my mother about the kebabs. You know we are not supposed to eat food prepared by non-believers. What was I supposed to do, starve?" She nodded, recalling tea with Manizheh after delivering medicines for her son.

"People were shouting their wares in many languages" he continued. "I thought I heard Turkish and Arabic, and there were other people whose language I had no idea about and whose clothing was different from any I had ever seen. Musicians played the *tār, kamāncheh* and *daf,* and sang with powerful voices. As the evening wore on, there were wailing love songs and pulsing rhythms of camel hooves, as well as storytelling and great exchange of news.

"One old woman told about the hero Zāl whose father rejected him as a baby because he was born with white hair. Have you heard it? It's from the *Shāhnāmeh.* My *Amu* Bābak tells some of the stories but I hadn't heard this one before."

Mitrā nodded again. "I've heard about it but don't know it well."

"Zāl was raised by the famous Simorgh, a magical bird who lived on a mountaintop with her nest full of chicks. She taught

46

him much wisdom and magic. They say she also scatters seeds and makes the land fertile. Later Zāl faced up to both father and king. His father regretted his foolish behaviour. I figured mine would not.

"The next day I went exploring the city and watched the builders at a new mosque. Tile makers on a scaffold high overhead were placing their tiles in the enormous dome. Many tiny pieces made up the whole, kind of like a carpet. One man on the ground told me that arranging the shapes of the small pieces is the hardest part. They must fit the dome and still keep the perspective when seen from far away. Workers carry the map in their heads, although I could see that they also had them on paper and that the pieces were marked to show where they should be placed.

"Soon I came to the bazaar. One whole section was devoted to carpet shops and I spent hours there just looking. Of course there are plenty of carpets in Yazd, but in Esfahān everything was different — the designs, the colours.

"One man was sitting out in front of his shop. He greeted me in a friendly way. '*Chai meil dārid?*'

"I welcomed the tea he offered and sat with him inside his shop. There was something about that man — he was easy to talk to. In no time I had told him all about my life, my father and my doubts about my abilities. Suddenly it became clear how deeply I wanted to make beautiful carpets.

"He nodded and handed me a book. 'Hold this between your two hands and consider your journey.' I held the book for as long as felt right and then handed it back to him. He opened it to a page chosen seemingly at random. The book contained poetry of the great mystic Hāfez.

Vintage Man

The
Difference
Between a good artist
And a great one
Is:
The novice
Will often lay down his tool
Or brush
Then pick up an invisible club
On the mind's table
And helplessly smash the easels and
Jade.
Whereas the vintage man
No longer hurts himself or anyone
And keeps on
Sculpting
Light.

"The poetry of Hāfez is beautiful but not always easy to understand. The man helped me. 'Ābtin,' he said, 'You *will* make beautiful carpets. That is a certainty. Your best designs will come from your dreams, from your conversations with God. Once you have found the heart of your carpet, the rest will fall into place.'

"His words warmed me through and through. I thanked him and went to say goodbye to the caravan, knowing I would continue on my way alone. Then I went back to the bazaar and spent the last of my money on more wool, more dyes and a good copper pot.

"Heading north, my thoughts turned to home. After all, I had learned a lot already. You were constantly in my thoughts, Mitrā, but so was my father. I could not yet face him and prove that I was a master of my craft. The journey continued — walking in the daytime now, weaving during the evenings and sleeping under the stars. I sold my belts and bags in villages or traded them for food. In the countryside, farmers took me in and fed me. Always I was eager to see what would appear beyond the next hill. Sheep were grazing, farmers were harvesting crops. In some places trees grew beside lazy creeks.

"There were good times and bad times. In the city of Kāshān, some children approached me in the bazaar, begging. It took a few moments to realize that all three of them were blind. How could that be? They looked like siblings. Had blindness run in their family?

"I asked and wished I hadn't. They told me they had gone blind working in a carpet factory where the light was bad and the hours of knotting long. At the end of a workday that started in darkness and finished in darkness, they could barely stand up. They had to work because their father was dead and their mother couldn't support all eight of her children. They were reduced to begging.

"I was outraged and furious. How could anyone treat young children like that? One day I will be the owner of a carpet shop. Certainly I would never treat anyone that badly. At the same time, a niggling voice told me that my father had not treated anyone that badly either, no matter how hard he had been on me.

"With no money in my pockets, I gave the children three of my belts so they could sell them. That meant missing a few meals but I was glad to do it."

Mitrā nodded. Her eyes never left him.

"Heading northeast, I passed a huge salt lake, all crusted around the edges. Luckily I'd been warned about the dangers of quicksand and didn't go too close. In summer when it is dried up, caravans cut right across, and I was lucky to join one. On the other side of the lake, you come to the *rāh sang farsh* — the stone carpet road. Shāh Abbās had it built when he walked all the way from Esfahān to Mashhad. It's like a stone causeway across the mud marshes. He was making the pilgrimage to the shrine of Imam Reza. Can you imagine the Shāh doing that? People said he did it just to show how devout he was but I was impressed anyway."

Mitrā couldn't quite picture it. "How did they get the rocks out there?"

"I don't know. After the end of the stone carpet road, at Dehnamak village, I continued alone. The worst time of my whole trip came soon after that. I'd been walking and walking and somehow lost the road, still thinking of those poor children. Parts of the road must have been covered with sand. Wandering in the *sahrā*, I'd eaten the last of my food a couple of days before. Hadn't seen a human being in more days than that. The water in my bag was down to just a few drops. Exhausted, thirsty, hungry and discouraged, I just wanted to lie down on the ground and give it all up.

"Then off in the distance I saw something — maybe a small hut? I went closer and saw an old woman come out. She was carrying a basin and in it ... could it be a chicken?

"I went closer and greeted her politely, '*Salām, mādar jun.*'

'*Salām pesaram. Kojā miri?*' she called back.

"That was a tricky question to answer. Where was I going really? I've never been sure why I answered the way I did. 'Grandmother, I am learning the art of carpet weaving. The plants, the birds, the rocks are teaching me.'

'Aha,' she said, 'you are having a conversation with earth, sky, water and all that abide there! Come in and eat.'

"I couldn't accept right away. After all, I was well brought up. I said the usual polite things: 'Oh no, Grandmother. You are too kind, you are going to too much trouble, I am unworthy of it.' And so on. You know how *ta'arof* goes, the polite talk. She played her part, repeating the invitation several times and at last, practically drooling from the thought of the chicken, I understood it was alright to go in.

"First she gave me fresh water. I thought about the old saying, 'In the desert a small sip of water is a blessing.' It was certainly true. The old woman cooked the bird up. We ate and once again I told my story from start to finish.

"I wound up staying there for several days or even longer. I lost track of time. She was quite elderly and alone. Clearly there were a few things she needed help with. The bricks in her walls and roof needed patching. I did that and then went out into the *sahrā* to bring back firewood — those dry thorn bushes that burn so hot. She showed me a spring not far from her hut, the only one for two days' journey all around. After that I brought in water every day and in the evening she told me stories.

"She took me out on what she called one of her collecting expeditions. That day, she dug up roots and showed me the kind that are good to eat, others that are good for medicine and still others that are good for carpet dye.

"At last, it was time for me to leave. As I was saying '*kheili mamnun, khodā hāfez*,' she gave me a little pouch, saying it contained a dye that would make a beautiful jewel-like blue.

'For your first carpet,' she said. The pouch had a symbol on it that seemed to be a talisman like one on her shawl. I was delighted that a second person had now told me I would succeed in making a carpet — and a good one.

"I walked and walked, again thinking of home and of you. How you would love learning about those plants. Would you be waiting for me, or not? Again, my father appeared in my thoughts. I was still not ready to prove to him that I was a master of my craft.

"Time passed. I met herdsmen and other travellers. One shepherd pointed out the great Mount Damāvand rising to a single snowy peak in the distance. Home of the gods and the Simorgh, that great mythic bird who had raised the hero Zāl. For that matter it was also the place where the demon king Zahhāk was chained, down through the ages, with snakes growing out of his shoulders. Good and evil all in one place. With the good winning!

"My weaving changed subtly after being with the old woman. Ideas simply came to me. I sang while working. It was as if the land was speaking to me. Then one day I found myself going up yet another bare, rocky mountain." Ābtin paused. Was this too crazy for Mitrā? But no, she was still with him.

"It was hot and I was tired but at last I came to the pass at the top. You know, if anyone had told me back in Yazd that you could see so many trees in one place, I would never have believed it. Spreading before me was a carpet of sparkling green leaves just beginning to turn red and gold. I fell to my knees to give thanks and then headed downhill. I came to a swift rushing stream and drank my fill for the first time in weeks.

"I came out on the flat lands. Much to my surprise the ground was so wet that people were growing rice! I walked on and came to a place where I could go no farther.

"If anyone had told me back in Yazd that you could ever see so much water in one place, I would never have believed it. Water stretched farther than my eye could see. That day, the sea was a calm slate-blue expanse. I gazed at it for hours and then saw a black speck off in the distance. The speck grew bigger and I saw that it was a boat. A fishing boat.

"At last, it pulled into shore close to where I stood. After a friendly greeting, the fishermen kindly invited me to share their supper. Their accent was hard to understand but when one of them held up a delicious-looking fish and said, '*Māhi*?' I got the idea.

"They told me the mountain passes would be blocked with snow, so there was no choice but to stay with them for the winter. I helped mend their nets and even went out fishing with them. It didn't seem to matter whether I was any good at carpet weaving or not. They just liked me for myself.

"It rained and rained. One of the men made me welcome in his home where I did my best to be helpful. I didn't want to appear ungrateful, or as we say, 'one who doesn't recognize salt.' I also made gifts for my sisters at home and gathered reeds that are supposed to be the best for making pens. And kept on weaving. It had taken on a life of its own."

The evening call to prayer rang out over Yazd. It was time for both Mitrā and Ābtin to go home. He drew from his pocket a simple necklace made of turquoise and offered it to her.

"This reminded me of you." She blushed even more deeply and put it on, turning it around, feeling its weight in her hand, and then tucked it under her *chādor*.

But she couldn't leave without asking about the beggar children. "Are there any carpet factories like that in Yazd?"

"I've never heard of any. Certainly not in my father's shop, and there won't be any such atrocities when I'm in charge either." Silently he vowed, Yes, I will be in charge. Why does my father not seem to realize that?

The next day Mitrā awoke full of energy. Her father was already dressed in his best when she came to breakfast. They sat around the *sofreh*, a special cloth they spread on the floor. Breakfast was bread, cheese and fruit, with tea to drink. Ahmad was going to city hall to meet the mayor and other dignitaries who would take the measuring cup and go out into the wealthy neighbourhoods to witness the opening of the gates.

Water flowing into private storage systems was carefully measured so that the owners paid the correct amount for it. Even though water was more plentiful than the year before, they still needed to be careful. The mayor, the *moqanni* and the water distributor were involved. They kept precise records on a chart in the city hall where the cup was also stored.

The measuring cup was made of metal and had a small hole in the bottom. They placed it in a container of water and opened the gate at exactly the same moment. When the cup filled and sank, the gate would be closed. If the customer asked for more water, they would empty the cup and start over, for the sake of accuracy.

"Where will you begin, *bābā*?" Mitrā asked.

"At your cousin Farideh's house and from there to other houses in the direction of the mosque." That meant that the home of Mitrā's former friend Maryam would be third. It still hurt that Maryam had not supported her after the *qanāt* collapse and that she would probably sneer at her today.

"See you there," Mitrā said as her father left. The measuring was a social event. Everyone came out into the streets to witness it and there was a lot of cheerful conversation. And gossip. She needed to go with her head held high. She dressed well although most of her efforts would be covered when she went out. Perhaps a bit of colour would show. Or maybe Farideh would invite her in and she could take the *chādor* off. Underneath she wore red, which always lifted her spirits.

She picked up her neighbour on the way. Haideh was a loyal friend and Mitrā appreciated it. Haideh had spoken up in Mitrā's defence when the gossip was at its worst and now they walked arm in arm. Haideh's family was Muslim but they had some Zoroastrian relatives, a branch of the family that had not converted to Islam when the others did. As they chatted, Mitrā found out that the relatives lived in the next village to Ābtin's.

Shirin had left with Ahmad and was already watching the proceedings carefully. As Mitrā and Haideh got closer, they saw a crowd was gathering. It was easy to tell who was on Mitrā's side. Some greeted her warmly while others looked haughtily through her.

Faraj!

Amu Bābak was still limping but cheerful. His wife rushed over to greet Mitrā while he smiled and caught up. But Bābak's face changed as he glanced over her shoulder.

"Don't look, Mitrā. Nāder Kermāni is behind you and he's staring."

"As usual." She tried to sound casual although she felt a rush of tension in her arms and her palms were suddenly sweaty. "What's he doing here? He seemed to have gone away from Yazd. Nobody knew where he went and now here he is back again. Why?"

Bābak nodded. "I wonder what he could hope to accomplish in Yazd now? Although people listened to his gossip, they didn't hire him to do their work."

"I wonder where his money comes from," Bābak's wife added. "He dresses well and has a good horse. Some people say he's taken out loans."

Mitrā couldn't resist looking. The Kermāni was staring at her with great intensity. She was the first to look away.

6

Zoroastrian Pilgrimage

The day before the pilgrimage, many Zoroastrians from Yazd and the villages to the south got up early and travelled to Sharifābād, a full day's journey north. Donkeys carried people, food and camping gear. Ābtin's mother, Sindokht, led the singing while Goshtāsp trudged along behind, grumbling about the state of the road. According to him, there were more rocks and potholes than the year before although nobody else noticed it.

Along the way, they took a short break to eat nuts, fruit and bread. As evening approached, they arrived at the village walls and entered the gates to a warm welcome from friends they saw only once a year. Sharifābād was the place where the most revered sacred fire was held, the *ātāsh bahrām*. Everyone wanted to spend time beside that flame, the great purifier. It helped concentrate a person's thoughts, which was something Ābtin felt he could use after the emotional upheaval of arriving home.

He and his family stayed overnight in an orchard belonging to some of his mother's relatives, who brought a meal to eat under the trees. They relished hot *nakhod du*, a stew made of spiced chickpeas, meat and vegetables. Endless variations abound all over Iran. Ābtin enjoyed the tomatoes, which his family did not include in the dish. Like Sindokht, her relatives loved to sing and laugh together, and they celebrated late into the night.

They were up before dawn. A good many people from Sharifābād joined the Yazdis on the long trip to the shrine, travelling together because there was always danger of bandits and wild animals. North out of the village they went, along the road to Esfahān. After a short distance, they left the road and passed over some low mountains and along a dry river bed, enjoying the beauty of jagged rock formations and fresh shade trees. In early spring, water would be rushing down the mountains through this riverbed but by July it was already dry.

Ābtin walked beside his mother, who was riding on a donkey. "Please tell me about the girl who saved *Amu* Bābak when the *qanāt* collapsed. What do you think of her?"

"I haven't met her." Sindokht replied. "But your Aunt Manizheh has. The girl came to their house when little Rostam was sick, bringing medicine that her mother made. She sang to him and even got him to teach her some Dari words. He got well when nothing else had worked. Who knows if it was the medicine or her singing and playing with him? We are all grateful to her family for the sake of Bābak and Rostam. The girl, Mitrā, is unusual. She loves those medicinal plants and spends time in the *sahrā*, even alone."

"Did she really refuse to marry a rich coffee merchant?"

"Most likely. There's another thing you should know. A strange man by the name of Nāder came to Yazd while you were gone. He claims to be a master water engineer. A lot of people doubt this and think he somehow engineered the *qanāt* collapse. Maybe he wanted to discredit our *moqanni*, Ahmad, who is the girl's father. It could be that — pure competition — or it could be something else. I don't know. He's also spreading evil rumours about Mitrā, even accusing her of sorcery. That, I don't believe for a minute. She's a good person."

Mother and son were silent for a moment. Then Sindokht turned to look at him. For the first time she realized how fully her son had grown to manhood during the year he was away. He stood tall, spoke with certainty and walked with the ease of one who has spent months travelling on foot.

"They are Muslims of course. Why do you ask?"

"No reason. Just curiosity." His voice gave him away. Even he could hear that his words didn't ring true. He went on. "I met her one day long ago at the *ab anbār*. I agree. She is a good person."

"But not for you, my son. Not for you." Sindokht shook her head sadly. She would have liked to see her son happily married.

True, they are Muslims, he thought. My parents would never agree to my marrying her even if hers did. Certainly Father would object. For some reason, he doesn't even like the fact that Bābak works for Muslims and is friendly with his co-workers. According to him, they should remain separate.

They sang along the way and rested under almond and fig trees. Some of the elders recited poetry and others told the story of Bānu Pārs, whose shrine they were approaching.

Amu Bābak started. "Everybody knows about the princess Bānu Pārs. She was the daughter of Yazdegerd III, the last Zoroastrian king of Iran. When the Arabs invaded almost a thousand years ago, the queen and two princesses fled northward from their home in Pārs Province, hoping to get to Khorasan in the north where they might be safe. They didn't get that far. As they reached Yazd, the enemy was gaining on them, so they split up.

"Princess Bānu Pārs came this way. With the Arabs closing in on her, she called to a boulder bigger than any of us, begging it to open up and take her in. The boulder sat there silent. We'll be getting there soon.

"Travellers hit that rock every time they pass, calling it rock of curses because it refused to help the princess. She ran on and at last, when she could see the Arabs getting closer, she prayed aloud to the mountain for help. It opened up and she disappeared."

"Originally the shrine was to Anahita," Sindokht added. "Before Zoroastrianism, she was the goddess of water, fertility, healing and wisdom. They worshipped fire in those days too, as well as the sun and moon."

Bābak nodded. "Now the place brings us sadness for all that we have suffered and happiness that the princess was saved from a fate worse than death."

Ābtin's sister Rudābeh was listening intently. She blanched.

Sindokht spoke again. "The spring is always here to provide fresh water, just as there is always hope. The water nourishes fruit trees here in the mountains. Our job is to work together as a community, helping those in need. We must build rather than destroy. It all comes back to the three principles: good thoughts, good words and good deeds."

As people began to disperse, Rudābeh moved closer to the older man. "*Amu* Bābak, is it really better for a woman to die than to be dishonoured?"

He thought about it. "Some would say so. I would not. Life comes first. For me, it is sacred, no matter how difficult. As far as the princess goes, there's no telling what the Arabs would have done with her. Maybe she was better off. What do you think?"

"I don't know," said Rudābeh. "Hearing that expression, 'a fate worse than death,' just made me shiver, as if I had seen the angel of death. I suppose we always have a choice, if we have the courage to make it."

"Just so," Bābak replied, wondering how such thoughtful children had come from Goshtāsp's family. They must take after their mother.

Food made the rounds. The young people went to sit under a tree beside a small creek where they were joined by visitors from nearby Zandju village. The guests brought fruit and a tasty dish they called *chaqu barizug*, made of potatoes, onions and eggs. They joined in the singing. After a short time, Ābtin went back and sat with *Amu* Bābak. He realized that his uncle probably knew Mitrā better than any them. He asked about her.

"I've worked for her father for years," Bābak replied. "He is a tough boss and a fair one. He doesn't tolerate sloppiness and he rewards good work. As they say, he's the kind with a giving hand, not a grasping hand.

"There's no way his *qanāt* could have collapsed from a flaw in the workmanship. I'm sure that sleazy guy from Kermān had something to do with it. I've seen him in the company of known thieves. If he is a *moqanni*, which is questionable, maybe he's digging them a hideout and taking a cut of whatever they get. It would make sense, given that he's got money and doesn't work."

"*Moqanni* Ahmad's family are good people and Mitrā is a very fine young woman. You know how she saved my life underground? She is brave and loyal." He gave Ābtin an odd look. "Is she the one you are dreaming of?"

Ābtin could only nod.

"Not easy," said Bābak. "You might have to go to India. Lots of Zoroastrians do. She's definitely worth the effort."

The day after the main ceremonies, Ābtin and the young villagers went to a place called *shekaft e yazdān*, which means cleft of the gods. Ābtin had never been there before and was curious to see what the crack looked like. When they arrived, they saw a narrow opening high in the mountain. It was a difficult climb almost straight up on bare rock. The opening was a crack only a very thin person like Ābtin could get through. A passageway opened into an immense cavern. There they stopped, sweaty and tired, looking around in amazement at the sheer size of the space. Their candles flickered. Ābtin was overwhelmed with an unbidden idea that it would make a good hiding place. But why would he need a hiding place? Only thieves used them. Besides, all the local people knew about it. Still, the idea of hiding stuck with him.

One of the local boys showed him a passage at the back of the cavern. Ābtin was shivering now and not just from the cold air. The boy said the passage led down to another cavern. As they got closer, they could feel wind rushing upward from within. Then their candle went out.

The local boy spoke softly in the darkness. "Ancient heroes are resting there. They are waiting for the mighty battle at the end of time. My uncle went down there once and saw them sleeping with all their swords and shields. He got really sick afterwards so we never disturb the heroes hiding here anymore."

After they returned to Yazd, Sindokht gathered the extended family and their friends to hear about Ābtin's travels since there had been little time for it on pilgrimage. She proudly displayed the beautiful bag he made for her, and his sisters were wearing their belts. With Sindokht's permission, Ābtin had invited Mitrā, who entered the house shyly. She greeted the family in Dari, "*shav do khash,*" and sat fingering the turquoise necklace Ābtin had given her.

She looked around. The house was crowded — women in colourful clothes, some with bright scarves over their hair and others bareheaded. The men's faces were leathery from long expo-sure outdoors. Clearly, they all knew each other.

Sindokht welcomed her courteously, and his sisters giggled and watched her with great curiosity as they passed tea and sweets around. They took their places on the floor. Rudābeh sat straight and tall while Katayun took the dog on her lap and played with his floppy ears.

"As you all know," Ābtin glanced at his parents as he started, "I signed on with a caravan last summer to travel to Esfahān. I thought I'd be back in a month, but ..." He glanced at Mitrā. This was hard. He couldn't speak in front of his father about why he had been gone so long — the anger, the yearning, the fear. "The trip was fine, except for one minor sandstorm. No bandits, Mother." He smiled at Sindokht, who always worried about bandits and wild animals.

"I did see one tiger from afar. Only for a fleeting moment. Esfahān was very beautiful, with the Image of the World Square and the tiled mosques. I saw the shaking minarets and walked across the bridge with thirty-three arches. You wouldn't believe how wide that river is. Wider than our house. Selling my weavings made me enough money to eat and stay at caravanserais. I went on northward alone."

Goshtāsp was frowning. Ābtin felt he had to justify why he hadn't come back then. But he didn't feel like explaining.

"I got curious about what else there was to see in the world. Mount Damāvand, for instance, and at last the Caspian Sea. Who could have imagined so much water? I brought back reeds to make pens for sketching carpet designs." He avoided his father's glare.

Surely there was more to say. His words felt inadequate. How could he speak of the light on the rocks, the man who had read Hāfez and made him feel he was worth something? How could he speak of that mysterious old woman who saved his life, the glory of snowy-capped Mount Damāvand in the distance and the fun he'd had with the fishermen?

People asked questions. Had he heard about any threats of war?

"Oh yes, people talked about it all the time."

How much were things selling for in the bazaars? He answered in detail. The guests laughed, drank tea and then went home.

How could a journey be so important, so life-changing and yet so hard to speak of? Certainly by now he realized how his family had suffered. All that time, they hadn't known where he was or when he'd be back if ever. He didn't want to hurt them further. He didn't want to make his mother and sisters feel inadequate, the way his father had made him feel.

That wasn't all. The sense of being alone in a different world was hard to communicate to those who had not been there. It was completely different from the journey they had just returned from. At the shrine, they had been in familiar places with familiar people and a common goal. His trip had been full of challenges, fear and excitement — and most of all, independence.

Things had changed at home too. His sisters were growing up. Rudābeh had already undergone her initiation and was wearing the *koshti* belt with pride. She had gone through it without her brother there to help her learn the prayers in the incomprehensible Avestan language. There was a new apprentice in the shop named Bizhan, about Rudābeh's age.

In retrospect, how could he not have seen how his actions would affect the family? Gone eleven months longer than he had said he would. Did he think no one would care? How could he say that it had been so necessary to be away from the family?

Soon afterwards, he and Mitrā met again. Approaching each other on the road, he felt they were being drawn together by magnets, just like that day by the Towers of Silence. Their smiles grew bigger as they came closer. Ābtin turned and they walked together. He asked what it had been like to wait, afraid to hear that she had suffered. He didn't think he could stand it. Did he make everyone suffer? She caught the look in his eye and told him that the waiting had been part of her destiny.

"Easy to say now that you're back," she said. "A lot has happened. You know about most of it. Of course it was hard not knowing, but I grew up and became more sure of myself." She didn't want to tell him just how hard it had been, going out to watch the roads, arguing with her father about marriage. As if telling him about all of that would break the magic.

"What made you decide it was time to come back?"

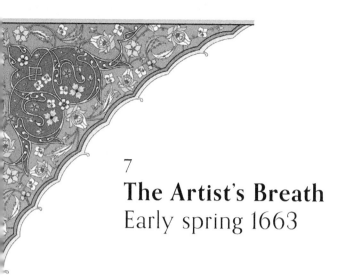

7

The Artist's Breath
Early spring 1663

"One night I dreamt about home — about Yazd. A girl was standing beside the Towers of Silence on the road out of the city. She looked like you, Mitrā, and she was waiting for me. I woke up in the morning and knew it was time to go home. Whether or not I had found what I was looking for. Whether or not I had mastered my craft.

"Back I went, across the rice fields, up the green mountains, fresh with new growth and blossoms on the fruit trees. Down the rocky mountains, already dry and dusty. I wanted to stop and see the old woman again and had made a special bag for her, thinking she could use it for her collecting expeditions. It was the best thing I had ever made, that was for sure.

"When I got to her place there was no sign of her and no sign of her hut — only a ruin of crumbled brick. I know it was the right place because there was a large boulder that you couldn't mistake for another — dark stone with odd white stripes in it. And the spring was nearby.

"I wasn't sure what to do. It was kind of spooky. Had it all been a figment of my imagination? But no. There was still the pouch full of blue dye to prove it. In the end, I left the bag beside the boulder as a kind of offering, just in case she came back."

Mitrā smiled inwardly, thinking of desert woman — the way she appears when we need her and disappears when we don't.

"Back across the *sahrā*, through the cities and villages. Even though I didn't see those blind children again, just being in the place where I had met them was enough to rekindle pain and anger about their situation. Through the sandy desert with its shifting dunes and up over the last range of mountains. Past the turn-off to the pilgrimage site and stopping briefly in Sharifābād. Everything was getting more familiar. Finally beside the Towers of Silence there stood a young woman. She looked like you."

Mitrā sat thinking for a long time before she spoke. "I'd love to travel like that someday."

"We will." Embarrassed by his own presumption.

"We will. It may be the only way to be together."

"We could go to India as so many have. It would be hard to leave Yazd though."

Mitrā shivered, realizing this was the closest they had come to acknowledging that they wanted to marry and knew how difficult it would be. Feeling uncomfortable, she changed the subject back to his story.

"I wonder if there's another way to express your experience so that everyone will see what I see when you speak to me. Is there a way to do it without revealing secrets or hurting feelings?"

Silence stretched. Then he remembered. "I heard a story one night in a caravanserai. There was a terrible war. In one of the cities, invaders killed everyone except the carpet weavers. Afterwards the weavers continued to make beautiful carpets and not one of them ever included images of war. 'Carpets,' they said, 'must be for beauty and tranquillity.'"

Faraj!

Ābtin went home and talked with Sindokht. "What do you think, Mother? I want to ask *bābā* if I can use one of his big looms to make a carpet of my own. I've had lots of experience by now and have sold many of my creations. A carpet design is forming in my mind. I think of it day and night. Do you think he'll agree?"

Sindokht poured the tea. As usual, she was wearing her indigo skirt and shirt. The only thing she varied was her scarf — today a bright pink with floral patterns.

"It is time. I can see that. The things you gave us are beautiful and well made. You have what they call the breath of an artist, a real inspired talent. You will have to approach your father gently though. He took it hard when you left home. Goshtāsp never would have expected such a thing of his only son. He doesn't understand how hard he is on the ones he loves.

"He thinks a man has to be harsh with his children — especially his son — to make them strong. Some parents can be strict while still showing the affection that lies beneath it. With your father, often the only thing you can see is that he's putting you down. But the affection is there, believe me. You may not have seen how proud he was at your initiation, when you first sat with the men instead of the children, even though you kept silent. When you were gone, he felt his life had no meaning. He was raving at first but once I even found him weeping. Can you find it in your heart to forgive him?"

She's always the peacemaker, Ābtin thought. *Bābā* weeping? Was that believable?

"Mother I am sorry I caused you distress, but …"

She took a deep breath. "It is not easy to forgive. Think of it this way. Have you learned from him? Perhaps you'll have to make the first step. You're a man now and the time will come when you and your father will trade places."

Of course, everything Ābtin knew on the technical side he had learned from his father. But …

"Can you ask him to help with some part of it while remaining in charge of your creation? That is the mark of a master."

Summer, 1663

One summer afternoon a few months later, Ābtin came into the workshop to find his father in a rage. "Where have you been? There's work to be done here!"

His temper was always worse in hot weather. Ābtin tried patience. "Father, I do work here. I also have my own work to do." Although not this morning, he thought, remembering the pleasure of his nearly silent conversation with Mitrā. Certainly more had been spoken with their eyes than with their tongues as they stopped in shady doorways.

"What work?" Goshtāsp sneered.

"What have I been doing this past year on the road? You know full well. I've been making items and selling them."

"You call that working?"

"I've made my living at it." He turned away, wanting to leave the workshop before he exploded. They'd had this conversation again and again in the short time he'd been home. With all these pointless arguments, Ābtin wondered how he would ever be able to make his own carpet in this shop. "You're like a bird with one foot, always repeating the same thing," he muttered. The conversation he'd had with his mother felt as distant as an elusive dream.

Goshtāsp was still ranting. "You think floors sweep themselves? That the customers bring their own tea?"

"I'm here now."

"So get on with it." Goshtāsp stormed off. Ābtin was fuming too, thinking he would have been happier if he'd stayed with the fishermen. What could be wrong with Father? If he missed me as much as Mother says, why can't he be a little kinder now that I'm back? I'm supposed to forgive him. Why can't he forgive me?

Anger fueled Ābtin as he worked. Rage made him precise. There was a loom to be restrung now that a rug had been completed and removed. He took great care with the tension and spacing so his father would have nothing to complain about. They used good cotton threads, the best. The knots would be tied onto the vertical cotton warp with a row of horizontal woollen weft in-between knotted rows.

He swept the floors into a frenzy of dust and noisily washed the cups and plates. Slamming the workshop door, he went up to his own tiny room.

Where to start? He'd had endless ideas for a carpet design on his way home from the Caspian Sea and even a few on their recent pilgrimage. But now? They had either flown from his head or grown dull, as if they were worthless. Camels seemed silly, trees ordinary, flowers sentimental. Was he influenced by his father's negative thinking? Where had the magic gone?

The only thing that still felt right was the blue centre — but what shape should it take? Besides, he'd be nearly halfway through by the time he even came to the centre. A painter or a tile maker could start in the middle and work outwards. A carpet weaver couldn't. Still, he consoled himself, when he made drawings on paper he could start anywhere.

Ābtin had saved enough money for paper and ink, and had reeds from Caspian Sea for pens. He could use local reeds for practice. There was something special about the way he had carried reeds all the way home from the north. He wanted to keep those for the final design.

Not wanting to waste materials, Ābtin went down the street to a piece of unwalled land at the edge of the village. It opened to the street on one side and to the *sahrā* on the other. The soil was baked hard, but there was a layer of loose earth on top. The houses were far enough away that he didn't attract attention. His dog, Rafiq, sniffed around and found nothing interesting. Why were they stopping here? He wagged his tail to encourage a move to somewhere with better smells but Ābtin just sat with a stick, making patterns in the dry soil.

Bits and pieces — never a complete design. There could be trees around the border, swirls of sand somewhere, although nothing shimmered in his mind's eye as it had while walking. He missed that sense of connecting with something bigger. The elders say all of nature is sacred. He had felt it while living outdoors but now …?

Ābtin imagined asking his father, "Where do you start?" He could just hear Goshtāsp's voice as if he were talking to a slow child. "Sharpen your reeds. Can't accomplish anything otherwise."

That's not what I need to know, Ābtin thought. I mean the design, where do you start your designs? At the centre or on the edges? Never mind the pen. What's the key pattern, the big picture? Do you see the colours at the same time or add them later?

But Goshtāsp wouldn't answer. He'd just say that his son was not ready yet.

That night Ābtin dreamt of the carpet seller who had read Hāfez to him in Esfahān and asked him the same question. Where do you begin?

In the dream, he saw the man taking great care with his tools, cleaning them and putting each one in its place, making sure the loom was perfectly aligned. Patiently he looked at colours and made tentative decisions. The master looked Ābtin in the eye and said, "I buy plenty of paper and, perhaps most importantly, I sharpen my reeds. All work is equally important. When my mind doesn't work, my hands move and find the way. The body knows what the mind forgets."

Ābtin awoke whispering, "The body knows what the mind forgets."

70

Mitrā found him later that day. Shirin came with her as far as the vacant lot and then went her own way, mapping two water channels she found in the nearby *sahrā*. One of them was not really a *qanāt*, she realized — more like a cave than a channel. Shirin approached carefully and looked in. Clearly it had been dug recently. There were a few bits of food inside and, oddly enough, a woman's scarf.

Something was wrong. For one thing, it didn't go anywhere, nor did it connect with any water source. What could its purpose be? More importantly, the place had an unpleasant feel to it. She would have liked to tell their father about it but that would involve explaining what she and Mitrā were doing out there. Shirin didn't want to get her sister into more trouble than she was already in for spending so much time with Ābtin.

Mitrā and the dog had reached an uneasy truce by then, aided by her gift of a chunk of bread that she brought him every time. Rafiq accepted it from her hand, which she quickly retracted. Ābtin watched, still amazed by their differences. What would it be like to have grown up without dogs? Without reverence to the fire? Would they have problems later on? Quickly he let that thought go. It felt like bad luck to think of things that were so far in the future.

Mitrā had also brought a worn piece of cotton fabric from an old *chādor*, a brush and three colours of paint. She had made them from plant dyes and oil: red from madder roots, blue from indigo leaves and gold from onion skin.

"I thought it would be easier if you didn't have to worry about wasting paper. You could play with these." She looked away shyly. "I've never made paint before so I don't know how it will work."

Her *chādor* opened, revealing her rosy cheeks, bright eyes and red dress with blue trim. "You're so beautiful!" Ābtin exclaimed. "I wish I could write a poem about you." He turned away embarrassed, so he didn't see the pleasure on her face.

He thanked Mitrā for the paints but doubted they would help much. What he needed was to see with his inner eye, which was not functioning now that he was home. At least, not while he was awake. Still, perhaps the body would remember. Maybe that was the problem. He hadn't done enough drawing for his hand to develop the habit. On the road he had just been weaving without first drawing the plan. That wasn't necessary with such small pieces and, besides, he didn't have any paper. Now he needed to draw more to sharpen his skill.

Days went by with Ābtin drawing in the soil, feeling his hand grow surer. Playing with abstract placement of colours on the cloth also helped, always with blue in the middle. He tried red on the borders with gold in-between. Or, as with so many carpets, red as a background with other colours for details. It was a good thing the madder grew so profusely.

Back in the workshop, Goshtāsp set him knotting cushion covers for one of his patrons. It was work away from Ābtin's own but he had to admit it was good practice.

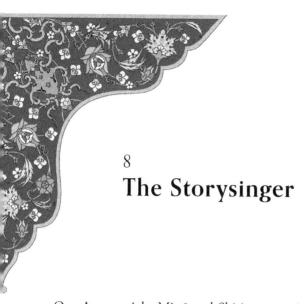

8

The Storysinger

One August night Mitrā and Shirin went with their parents to a coffee house to hear a *naqqāl* — a professional storysinger who specializes in the *Shāhnāmeh*. Now and then on winter nights, Ahmad would tell his children mythic and historical stories from this popular epic. Mitrā recalled the great hero Rostam's encounters with demons and dragons, as well as the times he had to rescue the king from his own stupidity. Although Ahmad told these stories rarely, he believed it was good for them to learn something about Iran's history before the coming of Islam. This night's performer was visiting all the way from Shirāz, so it was a rare opportunity to hear Iran's beloved epic told by an expert.

The men gathered in the courtyard garden behind the coffee house and inside the open door. Ahmad took an unobtrusive place outdoors since he felt uncomfortable meeting the owner. Coffee houses were relatively new in Yazd though they were becoming very popular. The man his daughter had refused to marry seemed to be doing very well indeed.

Women joined relatives and acquaintances who lived nearby. Places on rooftops or stone benches outside the houses were highly prized. Luckily for Mitrā, Shirin and Jeren, they had a relative who lived in a perfect location. They brought Auntie Golnaz gifts of sweets and flowers, and were welcomed onto the rooftop where they had an excellent view. Golnaz took the opportunity to point out several eligible bachelors in the audience below. Mitrā nodded politely.

The storysinger was wearing an elaborate vest with gold embroidery and a round hat with the same patterns on it. As he hung a large scroll behind his performance space, Jeren whispered that it was called a *pardeh*. The scroll depicted a man on horseback and a beautiful woman sitting on a rooftop, her long hair hanging over the edge.

It appeared that the programme had been changed. They had expected the *naqqāl* to tell the life of the hero Seyāvash and how he had come through a trial by fire unscathed. As it turned out, the evening's subject came closer to Mitrā's heart. The storysinger was to tell the story of the star-crossed lovers Zāl and Rudābeh. Zāl was the son of the king's champion, while his beloved Rudābeh was descended from their arch-enemy Zahhāk. The king would never allow them to marry. Many people, mainly the Zoroastrians, knew the story well and couldn't wait to hear how it would emerge from the mouth of this master performer. In terms of poetry recitation, the *Shāhnāmeh* was always magnificent.

The *naqqāl* set a large book on a table.

"What's in the book?" Mitrā whispered to her mother.

"It's his *tumār*. I've heard it contains outlines of all the stories he knows. As you'll see, he never looks at it."

Two young men came into the garden at the last moment and took places next to Ahmad. They exchanged polite greetings. Mitrā gasped.

Jeren whispered, "Who is that?"

"It's Ābtin." Mitrā was unable to take her eyes off him as he sat beside her father.

Faraj!

The Sheikh was dressed in ordinary pants and a jacket, a large scarf covering much of his face, and a hat with a wide brim and big feather. It was a disguise he used whenever he wanted to go incognito among his people. He liked to stay abreast of what people were thinking and doing, and knew they were always in awe of a senior cleric. The Sheikh, the most authoritative of any in Yazd, was leader of prayers at the Friday Mosque. His word was almost infallible, like an Imam. It would be intimidating for people to speak openly with him if they knew who he was.

He slipped out the back door and headed for the coffee house. The Sheikh was a man who loved literature and he kept all ten volumes of the *Shāhnāmeh* on his top bookshelf — as unobtrusively as possible. The pre-Islamic stories were not the kind of reading his colleagues would expect from a top Islamic scholar.

The audience quieted as the *naqqāl* stood before them. He began with a dramatic sweep of his cane, which Jeren called *assa ye naqqāli*. Several flashy rings glittered on his fingers as he gestured, making sure people were paying attention. He began with a ritual introduction. His voice was powerful, and every word reached their rooftop.

> *In the name of the God of life and wisdom, the sublime*
> *Entity that conceived us but can't be conceived, and in the name*
> *Of the one who is beyond our ken and above our space and time.*
> *In the name of the invisible maker of the moon, the sun*
> *And the constellations, who gave us wisdom to eschew evil*
> *And enjoined us to acquire knowledge and pass it on.*
> *Ponder these tales but don't call them fables or lies.*
> *Some of them conform to our reason while others*
> *Are truths that come to us in disguise.*

Mitrā was nervous. What would her father think of Ābtin? Oh please, let my *bābā* see how wonderful he is!

75

The story began with the hero Zāl's birth and his upbringing in the nest of the mythic bird called Simorgh. He grew up and was finally reconciled with his father, who had abandoned him at birth because he was born with white hair.

One time, Zāl was touring their lands and came to the city of Kabul. It was ruled by Mehrāb, who came out to greet him. They sat drinking wine while a minstrel sang of the beauty, intelligence and wit of Mehrāb's daughter Rudābeh. When her father came home, Rudābeh heard him sing the praises of the young Zāl. The two young people fell in love without ever seeing each other.

Here, the *naqqāl* took a break. A young man with a highly decorated leather basket came to the tables collecting donations for the performer.

The Sheikh looked around. His eyes stopped on Ahmad Moqanni, who was chatting with a young Zoroastrian man. That was interesting. So was the absence of the man from Kermān. What could he be up to while the whole town was enjoying poetry?

It seemed to Ābtin that he too had fallen in love without seeing his beloved, shrouded as she had been in fabric. Now he knew her face as he had seen it, first in dreams and at last in waking life. The man sitting next to him asked how he was enjoying the evening. Ābtin replied that it was wonderful and mentioned having heard the story of Zāl's birth and life with the Simorgh when he was in Esfahān. Now he wanted to know how the story ended.

"You'll find out. If I know anything about a master *naqqāl* though, it won't be tonight. He'll get us all back here at least once more." Surprised that such a young man had been all the way to Esfahān, Ahmad ordered more coffee and pastries and shared them with his neighbours.

The story continued. By now the listeners were thoroughly engrossed in the rhythm of the powerful poetic language, the master's movements, the way he used the cane, the emotional contrasts. The lovers met in secret and swore eternal love. Zāl wrote to his father, asking him to intercede with the king on his behalf. Rudābeh's mother scolded her for her scandalous behavior, meeting Zāl in secret, and then defended her against Mehrāb's fury.

The evening was over.

As they got up, the young man asked the older one, "Do you think they will marry?"

Ahmad laughed. "You'll have to come back tomorrow to find out!"

On the way home, Jeren asked. "Do you know who that young man was?"

"I do not," Ahmad replied. "But he's been to Esfahān. Nice fellow."

Jeren said no more, although while bidding her daughters goodnight she said, "Forget him, Mitrā. He's a lovely young man. Too bad he's not for you."

"He's so handsome!" Shirin exclaimed. "I hope you do marry him. And soon." She was thinking about her beloved Ali, the *ajil* seller. Shirin lost no opportunity to give her sister a hint.

The next day Ābtin and Mitrā met in a small market midway between their homes. He came up behind her as she was negotiating for peaches. She pretended to ignore him, although the fruit seller probably noticed the fire that connected the two. Ābtin picked out some apricots. Mitrā walked away from the stall slowly to give him a chance to catch up.

From there, they went to a bench under shady trees and talked about the previous evening. The *naqqāl's* performance had given them courage to declare their love for each other. They could speak of the story's heroes, knowing they were truly speaking about themselves. Ābtin began by quoting the minstrel who sang of Rudābeh's beauty.

"Lovelier than the sun. Lashes like raven's wings hide a pair of eyes like wild narcissus hidden there. If you would seek the moon, it is her face."

Mitrā replied with Mehrāb's words about Zāl, "As ruddy as a pomegranate flower, youthful and with a young man's luck and power." She went on with lines her mother had often recited, "How will we ever find peace unless we yield to love?"

They returned to the coffee house the next night. It was even more crowded than the night before since word had spread. So far Ahmad had said nothing about Ābtin. He didn't sit near him. Mitrā wondered if her mother had told him who the young man was.

The story resumed and the audience entered the *naqqāl's* world, full of Zāl's tension, anger and courage. He and his father Sām worked together on how to approach the king. They wrote him a letter, which Zāl delivered in person. The good thing was that both Sām's and the king's astrologers had predicted that if Zāl and Rudābeh married they would give birth to the greatest hero Iran had ever known. At the same time Rudābeh's mother Sindokht courageously crossed enemy lines to intercede with Sām, who had been sent to attack them.

A happy ending ensued. The audience in the coffee house and on the rooftops cheered, some shedding tears of joy. They knew this was just the beginning of a huge epic. Zāl and Rudābeh did indeed give birth to Iran's greatest hero, Rostam. Everyone was disappointed to learn that the *naqqāl* would soon be on his way to other cities. They might have to wait a long time before they heard such excellent renditions of other famous tales.

Mitrā thought about how the many names from the *Shāhnāmeh* appeared in Ābtin's family. His mother was Sindokht, his sister Rudābeh, the little nephew Rostam. His father Goshtāsp, as well as Katayun, Manizheh and Bābak appeared in other stories. Everyone who heard them loved the tales and identified them as purely Iranian, dating back to the era when Zoroastrianism was the Iranian religion, and even before that time. Hundreds of years after most Iranians had become Muslims, they still continued to celebrate holidays dating to Zoroastrian times. Noruz, the new year. Yaldā at mid-winter.

How could Muslims maintain parts of that culture so lovingly and yet object to intermarriage? Hadn't they cheered as Zāl and Rudābeh crossed a more difficult line in pursuing their love?

9
Rudābeh
August 1663

Ābtin had no time to think about star-crossed lovers after he got home. Everyone was upset. His sister Rudābeh had gone out to her aunt's house and not come back.

Sindokht had been to see Manizheh, who said Rudābeh had left several hours earlier. Where could she be? The worst thoughts came to mind. In these increasingly violent times, some Zoroastrian girls had been abducted and raped by thugs who claimed it was because they refused to cover their faces. Word spread and villagers gathered to search for Rudābeh.

Ābtin followed the route she would have taken to get home, ducking into dark alleys and stopping at the homes of her friends. No sign of her. He got home late. The family was sitting praying with empty, fearful eyes.

Mitrā had a sense that something was wrong. She paced, wondering what it could be. Not another *qanāt* collapse, she hoped, or more trouble from the Kermāni. Maybe it was just a mood she was having. Finally, as a distraction, she asked her mother about dye plants. "Could we make carpet dyes?"

Jeren could see distress in Mitrā's eyes but decided not to ask about it yet. She'd just answer the question. Mitrā would speak in her own time.

"Didn't I grow up in the mountains? Didn't we weave our own fabrics and carpets? Where do you think we got the dyes? Of course I know. We made our own dyes from plants that grew on our regular routes and I know most of the plants that grow here too. But it depends on the season. You have to plan in advance.

"August? There's not much available at this time, except that it's the best time for madder root. We can dig some up but we'd better get started soon. If we wait much longer it won't be any good. Then it has to be dried and ground to a powder.

"We'll want larkspur eventually. It makes a good yellow, but that will have to wait until late spring. Back home, it grew everywhere, but here not so much. We could also look for rhubarb to make the yellow. Onion skin works too, although its not as colourfast. He'll have to buy most of his dyes, if he wants to start before spring. We'll get the reds though. That'll be a good start and he'll need a lot of it. Indigo blue is a different story." Jeren was aware she was running on. Mitrā's pacing was making her nervous. "I'll tell you about that as we work."

Aware that she hadn't taken much of the information in, Mitrā looked at her mother, who was already packing the baskets for a trip to the *sahrā*. How could Jeren be so enthusiastic about this project if she really didn't want to see her daughter getting closer to Ābtin? Did this mean her mother secretly supported her? On the other hand, Mitrā also realized that anything to do with plants inspired Jeren, so she shouldn't get her hopes up too high.

Jeren always seemed to be able to read her mind. "You wonder why I do this with you? I told your father when we married that I must be able to go to the *sahrā* for the sake of my soul's survival and that I would live in a house but not be caged. Besides, as a good Muslim he can't question my charity. Sometimes he worries about my safety but still I must go."

"Do you really think we could be in danger?" Mitrā didn't think so. She'd always felt protected in the *sahrā*.

"Anything's possible. There could be danger in the city too. We choose our risks and balance them against the benefits."

Mitrā shivered.

"I still think it would be a bad idea for you to marry the Zoroastrian boy." Jeren had quickly changed the subject, and not for the better. "Nearly impossible. Still, you might as well learn about dyes."

Off they went on horseback, carrying their collecting baskets and trowels. "You can find madder almost anywhere," Jeren said. "It grows in dry soil and stony ground, as I'm sure you've noticed. Plenty of that around here. Madder also grows well where there are trees or bushes, and does really well along roads and at the foot of mountains. Just watch out for the prickly stems."

They stopped at a promising spot near some fruit trees whose leaves had begun to change. They dug madder root throughout the afternoon. Mitrā learned how to judge the plant's age by colour and size. Jeren said three to five years was best for dyes and showed her how to harvest the roots that seemed juiciest. They would wash them in buckets at home and cut them up before they got hard and dry.

As they worked, Mitrā sang softly, low in her voice, still sensing that something was wrong. The feeling kept coming back in spite of the work and the songs.

"Your voice is lovely, Mitrā. And calming. You have a talent for making people feel better."

"Do you think so?" Mitrā came back to reality with a jerk. "I sing to that little boy, Rostam, and come to think of it, it does have a calming effect. Even on me." She began to feel better.

"Daughter, is something on your mind?"

"Not really." She didn't sound convincing. "I mean, there is something but I just don't know what it is."

"You can always tell me." Jeren went back to the idea of singing. "The Sufis use music a lot, you know, to bring themselves in touch with God and the spirit in all of us. You may be finding that for yourself. It can open you to the feelings of others, which is not a bad thing as long as you remember who you are. Don't add their troubles to your own."

Mitrā hadn't thought of it that way before. It made sense that for her singing outdoors was as much a conversation with the soul of creation as talking with plants was for Jeren. Singing while playing with a sick child or waiting with an injured man could bring healing. These were things she would not have thought about a year ago. Now they were coming into focus.

They continued working for some time in silence. Was her uneasiness something to do with Ābtin or maybe little Rostam? Or a sense of danger she had never felt before?

"Indigo?" Mitrā reminded her mother, again searching for distraction.

"Ah yes, I just wanted to say that there are many kinds of indigo plants. What's most interesting is the way the colour changes when you pull the wool out of the dye bath. It can change from emerald green to a lovely purple blue in a matter of minutes. Nobody knows how it works except the master dye makers. It's a secret that has been passed down through generations and that makes it expensive." She shook her head. "Ābtin may have to buy his blue dye if he can afford it."

"He's got blue dye. Desert woman gave it to him."

"Really! She actually gave him blue dye? That means she must have thought very well of him, my dear. She helps people with information, food and water, a place to sleep. Very rarely does she give a gift that the traveller actually carries home. There may be more to your Ābtin than meets the eye!"

"Oh yes," said Mitrā. "There is."

"Still, it will be difficult if you want to marry. Your children would not be considered legitimate under Islamic law. Besides, the Koran forbids Muslim women from marrying anyone who is from another religion. You know that."

Mitrā hadn't known about the children. Nonetheless she replied, "Our children will be well loved."

Just then they heard a horse neighing. Nāder Kermāni was watching them from a nearby hill. Two rough-looking men were with him. Mitrā shuddered and her mother put an arm around her shoulders.

"Pay no attention," she said. "Let's hope that if you don't respond he will lose interest. His words and staring can't harm you if you don't allow them to."

"I don't understand it. He seemed to have left town and then reappeared during the water measuring. Now he's even more set against me."

Jeren knew he had spread rumours through some of the more superstitious gossip networks. "He talks to those who are easily convinced that a young woman who refuses a good marriage offer is up to no good. Most of them don't even know you. Nāder complains to anyone who will listen."

"As usual, putting forth the idea that I am making pagan rituals with plants. Always doing his best to sound righteous."

"Of course most people still support us. Friends of the family, Ahmad's colleagues and people who have had dealings with the Kermāni. All of them are concerned about your well-being." Jeren didn't add, although she knew, that most people thought Mitrā should get married as quickly as possible to calm things down. Ahmad's sister Golnaz continued to suggest likely young men to Jeren and Ahmad, hoping to make a match.

The men disappeared over the other side of the hill. Mitrā and her mother arrived home as the sun was setting, their baskets full of madder.

By the third day Rudābeh had still not returned. The search continued but the village was small. There were only so many places she could be. During this time Mitrā and Ābtin did not meet. Mitrā was busy helping her mother put her winter medicine stocks in order and could not go out. Ābtin did not venture into her world either.

Ābtin hesitated to talk to her about such things when she too might be in danger. Who would make the first step?

Arguments with Goshtāsp about his work in the shop continued. One day they fought over how much time he would spend in the shop at the bazaar, and another day, about when he would be able to do his own work instead of always being an assistant.

Everyone was on edge about Rudābeh, which seemed to fuel the discord. At last Sindokht intervened and urged father and son to come to a clear agreement. It was the first time Ābtin had ever heard his mother raise her voice. She was not going anywhere until things were resolved. She spoke and then stood silent, hands on hips.

It worked. Tentatively at first and then with more certainty they negotiated, decided and agreed. Mornings, Ābtin would be in the workshop or in the shop at the bazaar. Afternoons would be free for his own work. Somehow this uneasy truce stuck.

That evening Rudābeh appeared at the door, dirty, dishevelled, weeping. Sindokht took her to her own room and gradually the story emerged. Rudābeh's breath was rough. It was a while before she spoke and when she did, her voice was so soft that Sindokht could barely hear her.

"I was walking home. Three men appeared out of nowhere." She looked up. Sindokht nodded. "They were making insulting remarks about my uncovered face. Said I was asking for it. They came so close, Mama, and one of them smelled really bad. They grabbed me and took me to a deserted barn." Her voice grew stronger as she remembered. "I don't even know where it was. They tied my scarf over my eyes. When we got there they tore my clothes — just look." She went silent. Tears fell on the ruins of her favourite blouse.

"Did they rape you?" Sindokht asked gently. Rudābeh nodded. Sindokht put a hand on hers. "What happened then?"

"They left me alone, locked in the barn. I was just lucky there was a bit of water in a bucket. They didn't come back. Finally I found a way out by climbing a pole to the hayloft. It was scary but I jumped out from there. I was afraid they'd come back."

Sindokht held her daughter in her arms and let her cry. Then she heated water and washed her thoroughly.

"Just tell me this one thing. Did you recognize them?"

"Not really. Well, two of them I might have seen somewhere and just not noticed. They were rough types. They both smelled bad. The third one I would have remembered. He had a sharp nose and a thin face. His clothes were ... I don't know, just different. He wasn't a Yazdi. He looked mean, shifty. They took my scarf and taunted me, even threatened to choke me with it."

"I will tell your father. There is no need for you to tell this story ever again. We will do the rituals and then it must be forgotten. You've been both smart and brave. I am proud to have you as my daughter. You're home now, my darling." Sindokht was crying too. She would always ache from their inability to protect Rudābeh. The whole village would grieve.

Ābtin was uncertain whether he should tell Mitrā about what had happened to his sister. Surely she must have felt that something was amiss because of his absence. But would there really be any danger to her, a privileged Muslim? He had only heard of Zoroastrians being attacked.

He was surprised at himself for thinking of her that way. But after all, there was a difference. His thoughts were confused. He couldn't lie if she asked what was wrong. Why not tell her? On the other hand, wasn't it natural to try to protect her from such deeply disturbing knowledge? Mitrā wouldn't like the idea that she needed protection, as independent as she was.

It was nearly a week since they had seen each other. So far the villagers were keeping Rudābeh's story to themselves but, soon enough, the news would spread through the city gossip networks and Mitrā would hear about it. Even if Rudābeh's name were not mentioned, she might guess and that would never do.

The next day, still thoughtful, Ābtin stood in front of his father's dye shelves while Goshtāsp was busy with a customer. The man had come directly to the workshop to see a nearly finished piece that was still on the loom. Plump and cheerful, he looked around with great curiosity. "I couldn't wait," he said.

Ābtin moved to the other side of the workshop to give them privacy. Here, he saw that his father had placed some dyed samples on a work bench. He was determining the colour plan for a new carpet, commissioned by a wealthy family who had requested a predominance of green. Against his will, Ābtin could see the brilliance of his father's choices — the subtleties and the way one colour brought forth the qualities of another. The green of early spring leaves went well with the rosy pink, ivory white and a dark blue that Goshtāsp used in place of black. Each colour alone was not particularly dramatic, yet together they came alive.

Ābtin realized the colours of his own previous efforts had been amateurish, limited by what he was able to make or buy along the road. Even more, he was limited by his undeveloped eye. As time went by, Ābtin had improved. He could see that too. Still, there was a lot to be learned from his father. If only …

Now he took his reeds and a sharp knife and left the shop to go out into the *sahrā* to a place beside a large boulder about an hour's walk away. The empty lot was not far enough. Rafiq went with him. They passed through the village of Cham, where there was a huge cypress tree. Thousands of years old, the villagers boasted. Ābtin stopped and gazed at the tree, admiring its strength and size — no longer just a boring image. As he walked away, the tree took on a living power in his mind. He liked this place because the boulder sheltered him from the wind while still offering an expansive view of the *sahrā*, out of sight of the city and even the village.

His legs were energized by the walk and his spirits rose. He lit a fire using twigs and said his prayers. The fire helped focus the prayer and also offered a bit of warmth. Ābtin prayed that his sister would recover from the trauma she had been through. So far, Rudābeh mostly sat gazing out the window. She'd get started with some needlework and then just hold it, a haunted look in her eye.

Fury raged within him and he ached to find out who had attacked her. He figured the man from Kermān had something to do with it, especially after hearing Rudābeh's description. He started to sweat. Of course Mitrā should know about the possibility that Nāder Kermani was worse than just bluff and gossip. Never mind if she was a privileged Muslim. He had targeted her. Since his sister had returned home with her story of assault, Ābtin felt a huge rift between Mitrā and himself and was increasingly frustrated and angry, unclear how to cross it.

He got to work, carefully sharpening several of his practice reeds to be used as pens. At first he felt impatient, just wanting to get the job done and get on with more important work. Some reeds broke at the tip. Good thing they weren't the ones he had so carefully carried all the way home from the Caspian Sea.

Suddenly, he remembered his dream about the man who read Hāfez. The point seemed to have been that preparing the reeds was as important as making the design. Anger began to focus as pure energy for the work at hand. Gradually Ābtin fell into a kind of trance, enjoying the sound of the knife and the sharpness of the point that developed on each reed. Progress at last.

The boulder dominated the landscape and reminded him of the one near the old woman's hut where he'd left the bag he'd made for her. The image he wove into that bag was one that he'd seen embroidered on her headscarf. She said it was for protection. There's that word again, he thought.

The image was abstract. It evoked a man shooting an arrow from a bow, although it could also have been an oddly shaped tree. One evening she'd told him the story of Ārash, a heroic archer of ancient times. He was the one whose image was on her scarf, Ābtin was sure of it. Of all the stories she told him, this was the one that had stayed with him most powerfully — a guiding light.

10
Ārash the Archer,
told by the Old Woman

The old woman sat by the fire, warming her hands on a cup of tea. "It was a bad time," she began. "Good times were just memories that grew dimmer day by day. We had long lived in peace, enjoying the beauty of nature, loving each other, working hard with our animals and crops. We danced and loved telling stories and singing songs around the fire.

"But then a powerful enemy surrounded us, bringing fear and death. They came from Turan, to the east of us. Fear was so relentless that it robbed people of natural human caring and joy. That cruel enemy wanted to put our final defeat into our own hands and demanded that our best archer go up Mount Damāvand and shoot toward the east. Wherever the arrow landed would mark the border between their land and ours. Nobody imagined that an arrow would go very far.

"Later on, nobody remembered where the young man had come from. Ārash was his name. He seemed to appear from among us one day when people were gathered, whispering their despair to one another.

"Ārash told the enemy in no uncertain terms that he would challenge their bitterness and evil with his one and only arrow.

Our people listened to him. We gained hope from his courage and supported him wholeheartedly.

"He decided — listen to this, Ābtin — he decided to put his own soul into the arrow and then shoot. Ārash was fed up with death. He'd seen too much of it, poor boy, and knew it was the only way for him. I'm not saying he wasn't afraid. Who wouldn't be? But he realized his path had been determined. This was a cause worth giving himself to and he accepted it. He made rituals to the sun, moon, sacred springs and mountains, praying that they would share their strength and nourishment with him.

"Up the mountain the young man went — alone. As he reached the top, he was shrouded in mist. We couldn't see him as he let that fateful arrow fly, but shoot he did. We know that for a certainty. Carefully he took aim. His soul went with the arrow, guiding it and lending it power and resilience.

"After a few days, people went searching for him. They found the bow and the quiver but they did not find the arrow or the man. More time passed. Riders galloped out to the east. They came to the Oxus river and crossed over. After another half day's journey they saw Ārash's arrow resting in a massive walnut tree. What a victory! The enemy was called to the tree and, when they saw the arrow, they had to abide by their promise. From that day onward that place marked the boundary between Iran and Turan.

"And you know what else? Even now, when the valleys are snowed in, and travellers get caught and can't find their way, they call to Ārash for help. They hear his voice coming from the rocks as if those boulders had mouths. He warns them of danger and guides them on their way."

"Just as you helped me when I was lost in the *sahrā*," murmured Ābtin.

Watching as the sun moved across the sky and the boulder's shadow grew longer, Ābtin recalled how, down through the centuries, Zoroastrians had been surrounded and often attacked — first by Arabs and later by certain Iranian Muslims. He himself had experienced catcalls, the hated word *gor* — unbeliever — as well as fights and vandalism in a neighbouring village. Now his dear sister had been attacked. That experience would stay with Rudābeh for the rest of her life. The situation seemed to be getting worse although it always seemed to come from the outside, never from people they actually knew.

While on the road, Ābtin had neither concealed his religion nor shown it in obvious ways. Camel drivers and fishermen did not question him when they saw that he prayed at different times than they did or when he gave special reverence to the fire. He sometimes wondered if the old woman herself was a Zoroastrian. And why should things be getting worse now? After all, most Iranians had been Zoroastrians before the Arab invasion a thousand years before and some had converted much more recently. Not all Muslims were hostile. Take Mitrā and her family, for example. They were kind and fair.

Ābtin closed his eyes and saw the snow-capped Mount Damāvand, first as he'd seen it on his journey, and now as he imagined it on a base of jewel-like blue, crossed by Ārash's arrow. Damāvand, home of the ancient gods and kings — Anahita, Kayumars and others known by Zoroastrians and their ancestors. The evil King Zahhāk hung there in chains for an eternity, plagued by the voracious snakes that grew from his shoulders. He had been defeated by Kāveh the blacksmith and the young hero Fereydun. Both of them burned with a passion for justice and they acted on that passion. Perhaps they were among the heroes sleeping in the cave.

Damāvand. Good and evil in the same place with the good winning!

Ārash's one hundred percent commitment to caring for others was what won the day, not superior numbers or strength. He too must have been angry, and yet he channelled his anger into good. Ābtin's neighbours were like that, intent on finding his sister and comforting her. Simple things and large hearts contributed to victory. Small acts of heroism that meant so much.

His thoughts turned to his own journey. It was a success just to have survived and come back, to be certain of his calling and the love of a beautiful young woman. He'd had a lot of support. A cup of tea with the carpet seller who read Hāfez, the old woman who shared her food and wisdom, the caravan master who simply acknowledged him, generous fishermen who became friends. None of them cared about his religion, just his human qualities as he appreciated theirs.

But here at home? There were endless injustices in law and daily life. Not from everyone of course — just look at the gentleman who sat beside him in the coffee house. And why should there be such much injustice? Weren't they all related? He was angry not just with his father but with the world outside. Again he remembered the blind children in Kāshān and the injustice they suffered.

He would always admire Mitrā for sitting underground with Bābak, singing to him despite the danger. One of Abtin's aunts had said, "Love takes greater courage than anger." Would he ever be able to put his anger aside and help others with his compassion? He'd already begun to feel the transformation of anger into creativity. Now, as thoughts about who might need his compassion surfaced, his father's face loomed before his inner eye. He pushed it aside but memories kept coming back. Goshtāsp storming around the shop, shouting orders, criticizing all who came his way, eyes full of pain.

Ābtin would have to tell Mitrā about Rudābeh if she hadn't heard already. For his sister's sake, he hoped the gossips had not got hold of the news. He would have to face both Mitrā and Goshtāsp soon, with the courage of Ārash.

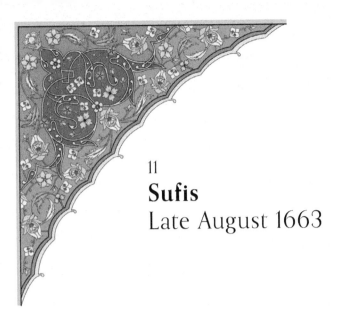

11
Sufis
Late August 1663

A few days after seeing Nāder Kermāni, Mitrā went to the *sahrā* with her mother again. This might be the last trip of the season since the days were getting cooler. Annoyed about Ābtin's absence, she hardly noticed the pure blue sky with its billowing snow-white clouds. Why was she always the one to search him out? She'd passed the shop in the bazaar a couple of times but it was always Goshtāsp who had been there. She wouldn't risk speaking to him.

She and Jeren dug up more madder root. Gradually the enjoyment of the land took over and she was able to concentrate on the madder instead of Abtin's absence. As the hours passed, Mitrā and Jeren moved farther apart, having decided on a meeting point for later.

Now that she was alone, Mitrā sang out with the full range of her voice. Much to her surprise, a voice sang back from over the hill. It wasn't her mother. Curious, Mitrā responded with a melody that fit with the other singer's. Back and forth the music flowed. Then she saw a figure come striding down a hilly path. This had to be a woman, although she was unusually dressed in mismatched bloomers, skirts and scarves streaming in all directions. She must be a Sufi.

"*Salām khanom*! Blessings on you!" the stranger shouted, still from a distance. Mitrā laughed and then bowed. She didn't know much Sufi poetry yet this one leapt into her mind.

> *You!*
> *always traversing the world*
> *searching …*
> *Tell me*
> *what benefit has come of it?*
> *That*
> *which you are seeking*
> *is with you,*
> *and you seek*
> *elsewhere.*

The woman laughed and came closer. She dropped her bag to the ground. "Good to find another person having a conversation with the Beloved."

"That's just what my mother says when she talks to the plants. She calls it a conversation with the soul of creation."

"Absolutely right!" said the Sufi.

Although she did find out that the woman was visiting a monastery just outside of Yazd and helping provide food for the poor, Mitrā soon realized she was the one who was doing most of the talking. She opened up to this strange woman and told her about Ābtin, his different religion and now his long silence, about the man from Kermān and his threats, her moments of despair, and her love for plants and singing.

The woman listened and then said, "Why don't you come to *zikr* some time? We sing, dance and pray. Things fall into perspective."

Mitrā asked to know more. "*Zikr* means remembrance of God," the woman explained. "We chant, recite poetry, make music and move our bodies. My name is Rabia, by the way. I took the name from a famous female saint. She's the one who wanted to love only God and really was the first Sufi to emphasize the importance of love. She wanted us to see clearly, without all the trappings of dogma, and she ran through the streets proclaiming she would put out the fires of hell and set fire to heaven. Do come!"

Jeren soon arrived and joined the conversation. "We can go together," she said. Rabia told them that *zikr* was held in a spacious house, which turned out to be not far from their own. Two of the teachers, who were called sheikhs, worked there with their students. One was a man and the other, a woman.

The next day Ābtin had a real windfall at the bazaar. A customer bought one of his larger bags with practically no bargaining. Weird. Nobody just bought things without trying to get a better price. The man seemed to come from afar, possibly Europe, since his clothing was unusual for Yazd. That could explain why he didn't understand how bargaining works, although Ābtin had seen him holding his own with one of the enamelware merchants so he must know something.

Ābtin decided he shouldn't question his luck. He took the money and went to buy paper. Enough to experiment with. It was expensive but, after all, the money had come easily. Why be stingy with himself?

Ābtin went home and started drawing the rug's centre. It made sense to begin drawing there even though the actual weaving would have to begin at one end. The carpet's heart would be a diamond shape with a stylized triangle representing Mount Damāvand in its centre. He played with curved shapes emerging from the diamond and placed the arrow across the triangle. Would it go straight or at an angle? Using Mitrā's brush, he added colour.

He began to hum and then to sing. Geometric designs alternated with rounded shapes. Perhaps a forest would form the border since Zoroastrians so revere trees — evergreens for immortality and pomegranate for their many-seeded fruit. Everyone loves trees, Ābtin thought, but in the desert they are a real treasure. Better yet, trees could rim the triangle just as they had appeared to Ābtin before he arrived at the Caspian Sea. Maybe a desert along the border? No, the desert must be one of the layers leading toward the centre. Camels for the border? Recklessly he drew plants, birds, huts and animals. After all, it was only paper and paint, not like a carpet where it takes months to see what you've made.

"Ābtin!" Katayun's voice came from behind him. He covered his work instinctively with one arm and looked up. The sun was low in the sky. Had his sister seen what he was doing? Would she laugh? Actually it would be good if she did since she had been so sad since Rudābeh got home. Their sister still sat silent, just picking at her food.

"Didn't you hear me? Supper is ready."

He grinned. "I'll be right there. It smells delicious!"

Much to Ābtin's chagrin, over supper Katayun told the family how beautiful his design was. Goshtāsp looked up in surprise.

"What design?"

Ābtin thought of the heroes of ancient times: Ārash, Fereydun, Kāveh. They had told the truth in more dangerous situations than this, although Ābtin's was a different kind of truth. In some ways, it was harder. Heart thundering, he took a deep breath and told his father how much he admired the colour choices he had made for the new carpet, their harmony and the way one shade amplified the other. Goshtāsp looked even more surprised. Something softened in his face.

Conversation meandered further and finally Ābtin said the thing he'd been practising for weeks. "*Bābā*, I want to use one of your big looms to make a carpet of my own — with your help."

Goshtāsp stayed silent a long time, his face unreadable, and then said, "Yes." Ābtin thought he would faint and then a rush of relief coursed through his body.

Of course that wasn't the end of it. The next day there was more negotiation about the conditions. Ābtin could use the loom as long as he continued to work mornings for his father, in the workshop at home or at the bazaar, and as long as he helped with work around home in the evening. He would not ask or accept help from Goshtāsp's apprentice, even if Bizhan offered it in his free time. Ābtin would make some practice pieces before starting on the large carpet. He could do that while perfecting his design and colour choices.

He agreed, adding the condition that Goshtāsp would help with colour selection and the overall carpet design but that final decisions were up to him. He knew this might be impossible for his father to stick to but it was worth mentioning. Predictably, Goshtāsp grunted.

Sindokht was always up before dawn, cleaning house. One day after morning prayers, breakfast and chores, she took off to visit her sister Manizheh. When she asked Rudābeh to come along, her daughter just sighed, "Not today." She hadn't been back there since the night she was attacked.

Sindokht didn't press her. Approaching Manizheh's house, she heard a beautiful female voice singing softly inside. She was shocked and taken aback to see that it was Mitrā. Her sister had told her about Mitrā's bringing the medicines that had helped put little Rostam back on his feet but Sindokht was surprised the girl would still be visiting now, months later. Was she just trying to get closer to the family? No, that was an uncharitable thought. Sindokht had come to talk with her sister about Rudābeh and was annoyed that she couldn't do it with a stranger present. It was frustrating but not the girl's fault.

Manizheh had beautiful wide-set eyes, which seemed even larger as she looked at them. Mitrā too seemed surprised.

"Sindokht *azizam*, didn't you know Mitrā is a friend of our family now? You've met before, the night Ābtin told us about his journey."

"Of course," replied Sindokht, regaining her composure and nodding to Mitrā. "I'm just surprised to see you here now that little Rostam is well."

"I came to love this little imp," said Mitrā, sending the child a smile. "Besides, he's teaching me Dari! *Sab bukheir*, Rostam," she said to him, and then turned to Sindokht. "Manizheh has been kind enough to let me visit."

Manizheh brought tea. "Sindokht, how is Ābtin doing now? Is he settling into being at home?"

"Quite well, I think. He wants to make a carpet of his own and has just convinced his father to let him use a big loom and have time to work on it. Of course he'll still work in the shop too."

Mitrā looked up, surprised again. "Has *agha* Goshtāsp really agreed?"

"Yes, just last night. We'll see how it goes."

Mitrā brightened. She didn't say more since she was unsure how much his mother knew about her. She'd have to see Ābtin soon, no matter what it took, and get the whole story. Maybe that would put her mind to rest.

She and Sindokht left at the same time and walked in the same direction.

"Mitrā," said Sindokht, "You have been a good friend to our family and my son holds you in high regard. Please understand that our religion does not permit us to marry a person from another religion."

"I do know that," Mitrā replied. But the look on her face told Sindokht that this young woman would not necessarily abide by anyone's rules but her own.

A few days later Mitrā and Jeren trudged through the fresh snow of an early winter storm to the place Rabia had told them the *zikr* was held. They'd invited Shirin too but she said she was uncomfortable with the ragged clothing some Sufis wore. Why didn't they dress better if they wanted to praise God? Besides, she was more interested in science than mysticism.

A woman opened the door and Jeren explained that they had been invited.

"All are welcome here. *Befarmayid.*"

Jeren and Mitrā knew that this would be an event for women only and that men would gather at a different time. The room was crowded. Many gave the newcomers welcoming smiles while others simply continued chanting.

Rabia came and sat with them. "Just follow along and listen with your heart. *Zikr* speaks directly to the soul."

There was poetry and music. Everyone danced, since movement is also an aid to communion with God. Hours passed and at last the woman who had greeted them came forward and began to speak. Rabia had explained she was a teacher who followed the Path of Love, inspired by the mystic Ahmad Ghazali who had lived in the city of Neyshabur hundreds of years before. Tea and sweets were passed around. Finally they said goodnight and started for home, talking quietly about the evening. The snow was already melting.

Mitrā was especially inspired by certain ideas.

"Passionate love of the divine releases the creative force. It sustains us and takes us home," the teacher had said. "Love is work. It alone can annihilate selfishness but this doesn't happen overnight. It takes practice. Love everything — the Creator and his creations — there is no distinction. Everything has a soul. As we search for God, we find ourselves."

"Some things are different from what we were taught," Mitrā said to her mother. "The Sheikh says that love of creation is secondary to the love of God himself. I like this better. Although, of course I respect the Sheikh."

"It only matters what you see and understand yourself," said Jeren. "It's the poetry that I love. And I've always known that plants had souls!" She laughed as if she were twenty years younger. Mitrā knew her mother would remember all the poetry she had heard. It was a great talent of hers.

"I loved the poem about the reed. I'll tell Ābtin about it if you recite it to me again when we get home. He uses reeds for his pens. I'll tell him how the reed flute mourns separation, having been taken from the reed bed and then gutted to make the flute that can sing. I love how the reed yearns for union. It's not just breath that will accomplish that, only fire. The fire of love ..." Mitrā's heart sank as she thought of the separation she was feeling from Ābtin. Why couldn't she find him? Why didn't she try harder?

Jeren sighed. It might prove impossible to keep those two apart. She knew Mitrā had suffered while stubbornly waiting for Abtin and that she would suffer again. Even now, something was amiss.

Gossip went on as usual. Mitrā avoided being present, visiting her cousin Farideh only when others were not around. Some days, her friend Haideh reported back.

"Not much is new. Simin's husband did not take a second wife and she is much relieved. But who cares about that? The gossips are talking about you and your mother now. Most are suspicious about a woman who rides horseback, works with plants so successfully and is outdoors in any weather. I told them it was ridiculous to talk that way. They just don't listen."

Haideh herself admired Jeren, while others turned up their noses.

A new rumour was starting — that the Kermāni had attacked a Zoroastrian girl. Haideh was concerned about her relatives and wanted to find out who the girl was. So far she'd had no luck.

"Maryam loudly refuses to believe the rumour. She still insists that the man from Kermān is too attractive to be evil."

Ābtin continued working on his design in the afternoons, drawing arrangements of trees, sand, camels and birds. He played with colour too, sometimes only in his imagination. Gradually the design took shape and felt good. He showed it to his sister Rudābeh, who gazed long. Her eyes came alive as if she were forgetting the horrors she'd been through.

"I'll help you with the knotting," she told him. He tried to pretend this was just normal. He was ecstatic to see this sign of life in her.

Goshtāsp's apprentice came in, bringing tea. Bizhan smiled at Rudābeh and she smiled back. There was more colour in her cheeks than Ābtin had seen in weeks.

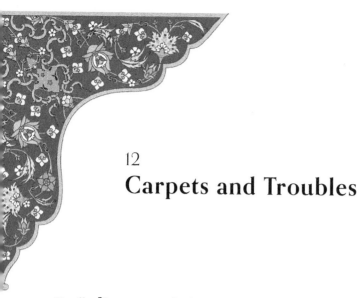

12

Carpets and Troubles

Finally Ābtin approached Goshtāsp with the design. He chose the time after lunch when his father was generally in a better mood. Ābtin didn't know that Sindokht had talked with her husband about this moment the night before.

"Start by telling him what's good about it. He's put so much of his soul into it, don't start tearing it apart right away. Then say what can be better. You need to let him make some of his own mistakes or else he'll stop listening to you."

Goshtāsp had only grunted, not wanting to argue with his wife. Surely he knew how to talk to an apprentice. Then again, did he know how to talk to his own son?

He looked at the design and was surprised — it was really quite good. He said so. Ābtin waited for the inevitable critique.

"The overall plan is good. Pleasant on the eye. But some of the proportions are wrong. You'll see when it's full size that certain things are different. Stay here a minute."

Goshtāsp returned with some designs. "See this? It's my design for the carpet we just finished." He was about to go on but caught himself and said, "What do you see?"

Ābtin looked. Sure enough, some of the motifs seemed too big in the draft. In the final design they were perfect, as he remembered they were on the carpet itself.

"We have to do it that way so we can see the motifs clearly, you see?" said Goshtāsp.

"It's like the tilework in the dome. I saw men working on a dome in Esfahān. One of them showed me how some of it had to look out of proportion when it was on the ground to get the perspective right when it's high overhead."

"Ah, I suppose so," said Goshtāsp, who had never seen tilework before it was placed in the dome. "We'll need to draw your design out on the grid once you get it finalized. Or we could do it now before you make any more mistakes. Do you have a grid ready?"

Ābtin ignored the insult. "Yes, I've drawn it."

Goshtāsp took the paper that Ābtin had carefully ruled in squares and began to redraw the design on it, precisely to proportion. After a while, looking at the blue centre pattern, he asked "What does the centre medallion represent?"

"Ārash the archer at Mount Damāvand. I passed there on my journey. It's so amazing, *bābā!* Maybe even grander than our own mountains, rising high above the others to a single peak that's always covered with a snowy blanket. It's a volcano, you know. Although it hasn't erupted for a long time," he added regretfully. "It would have been exciting to see."

Goshtāsp ignored the embarrassing fact that his son had been to places he hadn't.

"Ārash? How did you hear about him?"

Ābtin told an edited version of his time with the old woman, leaving out the part when he returned from the Caspian Sea to find that both she and her hut were gone. And he'd left his best bag there — just in case she came back.

Goshtāsp said nothing about the old woman. Instead he reminisced. "I heard that story about Ārash one evening when we were on pilgrimage, years before you were born. They say Ārash helps travellers who get lost in the mountains, even now. He wakes up when they call him." Ābtin thought about the heroes sleeping in the cave.

Goshtāsp went on to tell of the many times Iran had been attacked, even by Alexander the Great and Genghis Khan. "Worst of all were the Arabs. They imposed government and religion, and even tried to impose their language, although they didn't succeed in that, praise be to God. Often Yazd was spared by conquering armies since it was so remote. It took much longer for Islam to take hold but sometimes trouble came here too. It all depended on who the governor was at any given time. If he was intent on converting every last Zoroastrian, our people suffered. If he was a local man with Zoroastrian relatives, things would be better."

Ābtin kept quiet. Never had his father talked to him in this way before. Goshtāsp had to be thinking about the men who had attacked Rudābeh. He probably assumed they were Muslims, although it was possible they were not. Anyone could turn bad. That was one good reason not to let his anger get the best of him.

Goshtāsp pulled himself up as if he too had realized how unusual his talk had been. He looked as if there was something dangerous about it.

"Keep working on that design and we'll get the problems sorted out. You need more repeating motifs. More of those cypress trees I worked you so hard on." He winked as he walked away.

Father winking? Ābtin shook his head in disbelief.

That night over supper Goshtāsp spoke to his family with unprecedented formality. "Imagine, Ābtin has seen Damāvand! Did you know it's a dormant volcano? Of course we have magnificent mountains here with their own history, but we have never looked on the home of the ancient deities. My son has. A blessing on our house it is."

Silence fell. What had come over the man? He went on, surprising them again with a joke. "If only he'd woven a flying carpet, he could have taken us all there to see it!"

To everyone's surprise, it was Rudābeh who replied jokingly, "If I had a flying carpet, I'd take you right to the top of Damāvand non-stop so you wouldn't have to walk." Goshtāsp was famous for grumbling about the uphill hike to the pilgrimage sites.

Now Goshtāsp glanced at his wife and said, "It's time we got our son married. To a nice Zoroastrian girl." Ābtin looked away, gritting his teeth.

From that time on, Rudābeh was still often glum but there were more moments when she seemed like her old self. Any mention of their father riding a flying carpet was enough to make her laugh.

Ābtin reworked the design and showed it to Goshtāsp, who set him weaving just the centre of his design on a smaller loom.

"It's unusual," he said, "so we need to try it out." Then with great self-discipline, he stayed away while his son worked so as not to point out the mistakes before they happened. When it was done, he bit his tongue again and asked, "What do you see?"

Ābtin looked from farther away. He saw colour clashes and wrong proportions. And said so. His father breathed a sigh of relief. "You'll soon start to know those things without having to actually weave the whole thing first."

Late that winter, the design met final approval.

Accusations against Mitrā had calmed down for several months, but as spring approached they returned, like weeds with the flowers. Mysteriously, animals had begun to die. Nāder spread rumours that Mitrā had been cursing people she didn't like, which was ridiculous since just as many animals belonging to her friends had died as those belonging to others. What was worse was that he also included Jeren and Shirin in his accusations.

Again he went to the Sheikh, who refused to talk to the him. Everything that needed saying had been said the first time, he thought. The man was a nuisance — or something even worse. He needed watching.

Mitrā continued to go out, often with Shirin and their neighbour Haideh, sometimes with her mother or her aunts and cousins. Once she even went with her Sufi friend Rabia, delivering food to the poor. Mitrā's brother, Mahmood, occasionally accompanied her to the bazaar, although she tried to avoid excursions with him since it was hard to slip away from his watchful eye.

Once in a while she ventured out alone, although there was a great hue and cry against that among her relatives. "Keep that girl under lock and key," Uncle Hossein said to her father. "Her name may be ruined but please, Ahmad, we all love her and she is in danger."

"Didn't you teach her any decency?" moaned Aunt Golnaz. Her efforts to match Mitrā with various young men were not succeeding and yet she never gave up.

"Try harnessing the whirlwind, my dear brother. She has a very decent heart, Golnaz." Ahmad didn't want to see his daughter secluded in fear, but he too urged caution, both for her safety and for the family's reputation.

Stories had circulated about Zoroastrian girls who had been attacked although still no names had been mentioned.

"Don't ever go out alone," Ahmad urged.

As usual, Mitrā went out delivering medicines and doing the family's shopping. She often found ways to stop at the bazaar where there was still no sign of Ābtin. Finally one day she could no longer deal with the silence and managed to convince Shirin and Haideh to go home from the bazaar without her.

"I'll be back in time for evening prayers." Mitrā went on to the village and to Ābtin's home, bringing sweets to go with the family's afternoon tea.

She couldn't help noticing that Rudābeh did not look well. Could this be the problem? At last Ābtin came into the room, stopping when he saw Mitrā and greeting her more formally than usual. She asked if he wanted help putting the wool in order in the workshop. They went out together.

"What is the matter, Ābtin?" she asked. "I haven't seen you in so long. Is Rudābeh ill? She doesn't look well."

This was the moment. He had to tell her what had happened. All of it — the abduction, the search and at last her homecoming — that she had been dishonoured, since he couldn't speak any other word for it.

"That's why we haven't seen each other. I couldn't figure out how to tell you. She's feeling much better now than she was," he concluded. Then Ābtin added the description Rudābeh had given of the two thugs and the man who looked like the Kermāni.

Mitrā stared at him in disbelief. How could such a thing happen here — and to someone she knew? It was an outrage. Tears sprang to her eyes. A picture of Nāder Kermāni flashed in her mind and the way he had looked at her. He must be much worse than she had imagined. She didn't know what to say and neither did Ābtin.

Suddenly Mitrā realized it was nearly time for evening prayers. "I've got to go," she announced and immediately started to put on her outdoor clothing. Then she hurried back and hugged Rudābeh silently.

"You can't go alone," said Ābtin. "Not after what's happened. I'll go with you."

Normally Mitrā would have said she'd be perfectly safe but now she realized she really wanted the company. He too prepared to go out, calling Rafiq to go with them. As they passed through the courtyard, the apprentice Bizhan joined them.

A couple of homeless dogs followed them cautiously through the village. People called them lane dogs and often fed them. By now, like most of the village dogs, they knew Mitrā.

They crossed the barren lands into Yazd just as the sky was turning purple. The sun cast deep shadows on rocks and bushes, filling their colours with mystery. They passed the bazaar and went off into an alley that led to a small square not far from Mitrā's home. There was hardly anyone around. Silence reigned until the call to prayer emerged from a nearby mosque. The muezzin's rich voice spread in all directions, calming the rush of daily activity with its deep, resonant tones and inviting people to commune with the sacred.

"Hey, there's the witch!" Five boys, all a few years younger than Ābtin and Mitrā, came out of an alley. They were about Bizhan's age and dressed as if they were coming from the *madraseh*, the religious school.

A second boy laughed loudly. "How can you tell?"

"I've seen her before. My mother pointed her out. You can tell by her shoes and her immodest walk. And here she is with two of the *gor* and their unclean animals. There's one way to be sure though. Witches have marks on their necks." He rushed forward and tore at Mitrā's *chādor*. She slapped him and then there was a melee. The city boys were smaller but strong, and there were more of them.

The next thing she knew, they had Ābtin and Bizhan down on the ground and were punching and scratching them. Ābtin and Bizhan struggled to get up, and Mitrā grabbed at the boys, trying to pull them off. Rafiq barked. The lane dogs, who were still following some distance behind them, came rushing to the rescue, snarling and barking furiously. One dog bit the boy who had started it all on the leg. He cried out and then they were all running away, boys one way and dogs the other.

The three hurried on to Mitrā's house but the young men refused to come in beyond the entranceway. They were dishevelled and Ābtin's arm was bleeding.

"Stay here," said Mitrā, "We'll clean you up."

She went for Jeren, who came quickly with water, rags and salve, and cleaned their wounds. She too invited them in but they thanked her politely for her help and headed for home. Jeren checked Mitrā over too, finding nothing more than a few bruises and a torn *chādor*. Now that it was over, Mitrā burst into tears and Jeren took her in her arms.

"I'll break this to your father gently," she said. "He will be furious with the boys for harassing you and with you for being out, and with himself for not being there there to protect you. Did you recognize any of the boys?"

"Two of them," Mitrā gulped and named two boys who lived nearby.

"Your father will have a word with their parents. Oh, to think that our city could come to this."

Mitrā would have to tell mother about Ābtin's sister soon but not now. Why? Was it just too horrible? Maybe she didn't quite believe it herself yet. Her parents would get a lot stricter about her going out if they knew, which was understandable although unlikely to stop her. At the same time, her sense of safety was crumbling. She should tell Shirin and Haideh for their own safety and couldn't face that either.

Sleep would not come.

Ahmad talked to the boys' parents. "They owe her an apology," he said. "Those boys need to learn respect for their neighbours. The Sheikh would be highly displeased if he heard of such goings-on, and so close to the mosque that reminds us of God's compassion."

The boys got a severe talking-to, although one of the fathers told Ahmad he should keep better control of his women, adding that the Sheikh would also be displeased to hear of the girl's behaviour and choice of company. This annoyed Ahmad but he warned Mitrā more strongly than before. A few days later, the boys came and gave her an insincere apology.

One morning not long after that, Jeren told Mitrā, "Your father is taking a gift to Ābtin to thank him for taking care of you. It was a risk for him, you know. The same people who don't like you also don't like Zoroastrians, especially when they bring their dogs into our neighbourhood."

Mitrā was amazed. Her father, going to thank Ābtin? She would try to be more careful, although she wouldn't give in to fear.

Gossip continued even more emphatically than before. Some people were saying that Nāder had raped a Zoroastrian girl. Maryam insisted he could not have been the one and that he had been seen elsewhere. She was still taking his side although it was getting harder.

On the other hand, who knew exactly when it had taken place or even who the girl was? Mitrā had told Haideh by now but neither of them had told anyone else. There was no certainty about any of it. At first, Nāder had always been seen alone, although later he had appeared several times with two rough-looking characters, known thieves who were said to have stolen not only from houses and shops but also from a mosque.

The gossips also debated where Nāder's money could have come from.

"He still dresses well and rides a fine horse although nobody hires him to work."

"He must be taking loans. Just watch, soon the creditors will be after him."

"If he is working with thieves, maybe he has another source of income — an illegal one."

Opinions were divided about the boys who had attacked Mitrā. The majority asked pointedly why she had been out with two Zoroastrian men and their dogs. Others, encouraged by Haideh, said there was no excuse for the boys' behaviour no matter what Mitrā was doing.

One day Mitrā saw the man from Kermān in the bazaar. This time, he came right up to her while her mother was busy negotiating for some sweets. He whispered words she didn't quite catch although his threatening tone was clear. He glared at her mother too but was gone by the time Jeren turned around.

Ābtin was alone in the shop when a man came in, the one who had sat next to him at the coffee house. He greeted the man with the traditional formulas of polite speech, saying it was a pleasure and an honour to see him again. The man returned the *ta'arof* and accepted a cup of tea. After a few words about the excellence of the performance they had seen, he spoke about Ābtin's father's work. "Very beautiful. Goshtāsp is a master. Are you his son? You must be following in his footsteps."

"I am doing my best, learning from him and finding my own art," Ābtin replied.

"Just so." Ahmad seemed to be taking something in beyond Ābtin's words. He tactfully changed the subject and came to the point. "I am Ahmad Moqanni. I've come to thank you for helping my daughter, Mitrā. Please accept a simple gift from her mother and me." He reached into his bag and took out a hat. It was slightly dome-shaped, made of velvet with embroidered cypress images in four colours. Flaps turned up at the sides.

At last Ābtin found his tongue. "It was nothing really. Anyone would have done the same. You are doing me too much of an honour. I am not worthy of it."

"No *ta'arof* now. This is no time for modesty. You were courageous and may have saved her from a bad beating. I have spoken to her. From now on, she must be much more careful."

Ābtin placed the hat carefully on his head and smiled. "I'm grateful to you."

"I am pleased to have met you again. Blessings upon you." And then the man was gone.

That evening, Mitrā's parents sat together. "Why should we say no?" said Jeren. "After all, our own marriage went against convention and has been a good one."

"*Azizam*, we live in a different time now. Violence in the streets? And it's not only children. Besides, marriage between a Muslim woman and a Zoroastrian man goes against our Islamic *Sharia* law. Who would perform the ceremony? You believe it is her destiny to bring people together." They sat in silence for a few minutes and then he went on. "You may be right. We do our best to protect our children but their path is their own. The truth is I don't know what to do."

Ābtin and his father continued working together, taking turns looking at the written plan and calling out which colours would come next. This made the knotting go much faster. They checked the evenness of the knots, matching details. Father and son still argued occasionally but there were moments when they worked comfortably in silence.

Mitrā and Jeren went to *zikr* a second time. The teacher spoke about how the cosmos is inside us, not outside, and about the power of love.

"Sometimes love overwhelms people," she said, "and then allows them courage and strength they would not have found otherwise."

Mitrā thought of Ābtin's fighting on her behalf. He hadn't stopped to think it over. Nor had she, when climbing down into the *qanāt* to be with Bābak. Nor had Rudābeh when she jumped from the hayloft.

"The goal of our work is unity," the teacher said. "How can we believe in one God if we cannot find unity in ourselves?"

One poem Mitrā heard that night spoke eloquently of the love that surpasses dogma.

> *I will incinerate this creed and religion, and burn it.*
> *Then I will put your love in its place.*
> *How long must I hide*
> *this love in my heart?*
> *What the traveller seeks*
> *is not the religion*
> *and not the creed:*
> *Only You.*

If there is just one God, why don't we recognize the deity in ways other people understand? Mitrā knew that this poem spoke of God. It seemed also to speak to her situation.

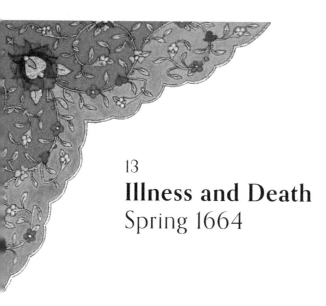

13
Illness and Death
Spring 1664

As time went by, the disease got worse. Not just animals, people were catching it now. Frighteningly, healthy adults and children were dying in just a few days. Stories from hundreds of years back were revived. There was talk of the Black Death that had come to Yazd from farther north. It first came to Iran with the Mongols or along the trade routes, carried on straw infested with rats and fleas. However it arrived, it brought disaster. Many believed it was the strong hand of fate punishing the wicked, controlled by sorcerers. This felt like a return of the plague although the symptoms were not the same.

Ābtin's father fell ill. He lay on his bed day and night, sweating with fever, moaning and cursing fate. Mitrā and Jeren kept their faces more tightly covered than usual as they passed through the streets, bringing him medicine. They sat by the hour with Goshtāsp who looked so much older now, and helpless.

Mitrā sang to him. As he grew still weaker, she felt hopeless. Nothing seemed to help this man who had inspired fear, resentment and grudging admiration from those close to him.

"It's my bad fate. Good family, just me with my own destiny," he croaked, stopping frequently to cough. "Started back when I was a boy. I wanted to study, maybe become a priest … but then my older brother disappeared from our lives. I was next oldest and had to give up my own dreams and take over the carpet shop … My mother was the one with real talent, the real artist's breath and technique. She taught me but I never reached her greatness. Would have done better financially if I'd converted to Islam but that was something I vowed never to do. Nor will my son." He gave Mitrā a stern look.

She wondered what had happened to his brother but didn't ask. Now she could see where Goshtāsp's fears for his son had come from. Was he afraid that Ābtin would convert to Islam because of her? Did he fear that his son would become greater than he was?

"Don't worry," she said. "He won't convert."

Ābtin took over the shop. He made small carpets and bags, and finished a few of Goshtāsp's projects. Although the customer who had ordered the green carpet expressed patience and sent best wishes to the ailing carpet weaver, certainly the job needed to be completed. Ābtin began overseeing the work of Bizhan and a new apprentice. He called out the colours as they worked. They developed a good rhythm and the work went quickly.

One day as Ābtin sat with his ailing father, telling him how well the green carpet was coming along, Goshtāsp coughed and whispered, "Get on with your own work, son. You have a good eye, you've practised, you are ready. Take my place."

Ābtin found himself weeping, unsure if it was from the thought of his cranky old father dying or from having received the acknowledgement he had always longed for. It came so simply and unexpectedly, at a moment when his thoughts were elsewhere, and he felt no anger for the old man.

"Don't worry, father," he said. "We'll carry on your lineage."

Ābtin set up the loom he was to use for his own carpet and made the final choices of colour. The main background would be madder red. White, green and a dark blue featured strongly. Yellow was downplayed, since Zoroastrians considered it unlucky. The desert was represented by a light brown, and of course the centre would be the old woman's jewel-like blue, standing out from the darker blue of the carpet's corners. Most of the wool was dyed. He drew the design one last time, showing precisely where the knots would change colour.

He began knotting alone. It was slow going since he had to be constantly consulting the plan. Some days Mitrā or Katayun came and sat with him, calling the colours. When Bizhan offered to help, Ābtin had to say no, since he had agreed with his father that he would not use the apprentices for his own work. Still, Bizhan helped out in unobtrusive ways, cleaning up and replenishing supplies when needed.

Goshtāsp was recuperating slowly. Although he was nowhere near his old strength, they were glad he was not among those who had died from the mysterious illness. He stayed mostly in the house, although occasionally he came out for a breath of spring air. Noruz came and went with little celebration.

By mid-summer the carpet had reached the place where the jewel-like blue centre would begin. Carefully Ābtin opened the pouch the old woman had given him. Immediately he smelled the pungent *sahrā* herbs that grew where she lived. The aroma took him back to the day he had almost given up and she had saved him. He saw the rolling landscape with its occasional jagged rocks. He felt the fresh breezes and the taste of cool water from the spring. His hands felt the dry warmth of hers as she gave him the pouch. Once the wool was dyed, they continued knotting. The centre came out even more beautifully than he could have imagined, radiating warmth and mystery.

One hot sunny day when the centre medallion was about halfway done, Goshtāsp insisted on walking to the workshop to see how it was coming along. He was still bent over a bit and he carried the bag Ābtin had made for him, although there seemed to be nothing in it. This was the farthest he had walked since becoming ill. He looked around, noting the spic and span condition of the shop and some smaller pieces in progress on looms worked by the apprentices. Ābtin imagined Goshtāsp was almost sorry there was nothing to complain about, as if his father felt he was no longer needed.

He checked Ābtin's knotting and nodded. "Good — tight and even." Ābtin watched his father limp around the front of the loom, examining the carpet from different directions. At last he pulled himself up and looked his son in the eye. "You take after your grandmother." This was high praise indeed. Ābtin's grandmother had been highly respected as a carpet weaver, the kind with a true inspiration that some people called *fut o fan*, meaning the artist's breath and technique. She had true inspiration and long-practised skills.

Ābtin felt tears pricking against his eyelids. Was this emotion at the heart of the carpet — the place the man in Esfahān had spoken of?

Goshtāsp turned on one heel and leaning on his cane, left the workshop. Ābtin heard him coughing as he made his way slowly back to the house. That night the old man's fever returned.

Three days later a priest dressed in white with a veil covering his nose and mouth came to the house. He prayed with the dying man. Sindokht was outside the door, feeding the dog. Ābtin was bringing in firewood while other relatives sat chatting nearby. At just that moment, when no one was looking, Goshtāsp's soul left his body. Sindokht wept loudly, joined by her two daughters. Two of Goshtāsp's three brothers were there, and they wept with Ābtin, putting their arms around each other.

Ābtin felt badly, thinking he had pushed his father beyond his limits by letting him walk to the workshop. But his mother reassured him. "He was waiting to be sure the lineage would carry on. You gave him what he needed and then he was able to go."

There were things that had to be done right away. A body without its soul could not stay long in the house as it was now impure and might contaminate others. In the meantime, someone always sat with the body, keeping the fire going. Rafiq stayed loyally nearby, guarding the body. Rudābeh brought coals and placed them in a metal bowl near her father's body. Special herbs were used to clear the air. Uncle Fereydun sent Ābtin to find the men who made a profession of laying out male bodies. Of course, if a woman had died, it would be a woman who did this job.

After speaking to the men, Ābtin sent two boys with a message for Mitrā, saying that his father had left the world. He wouldn't neglect telling her what had happened. He wouldn't make that mistake again.

The men came quickly, since they had known that Goshtāsp might go at any moment. They connected themselves with a woven *koshti* belt and set to work, washing the body and dressing it in clean clothes.

Ābtin was numb, shocked that this man who had been so vital, even terrifying, could be gone. Disconnected thoughts flashed through his head about what would happen now, about the responsibilities that would come to him as the only son of the family.

By mid-afternoon, the whole village knew and people gathered to accompany the family to the Towers of Silence. Some stood quietly outside the house, murmuring prayers. Others entered bearing gifts of *halva sen*, made of rice or wheat that had been cooked down in oil and seasoned with sugar and saffron.

It would be a long walk to the Towers, especially for those carrying the heavy metal bier. Plenty of men were there, prepared to spell each other with the weight. The professional bearers, all dressed in white, gave instructions. Others who joined the procession connected themselves with *koshti* belts. Neighbourhood dogs also gathered, eager to go on any excursion but seeming to understand the solemnity of this one.

As they were about to set off, Mitrā appeared with Jeren. They sought out Ābtin's mother to offer their condolences and ask if they might join the walk to the Towers. Sindokht looked them up and down, and then seemed to make an internal decision.

"Of course you are welcome," she said. "Do you understand the ceremony? We stop outside the Towers. Only the bearers go in."

"We will follow your lead, *khanom*," said Jeren politely. When they joined the line, some people moved away from them but others came and tied them in.

At first, the walk seemed endless with countless stops for more prayers along the way. They passed the village, houses closed and the bazaar empty as everyone joined the procession. The road opened — first gardens appeared and soon there was nothing but barren land with just a few thorn bushes growing. As dust rose from the road, Mitrā thought back to the times she had gone to the Towers to wait for Ābtin — the uncertainty, her joy when he finally appeared. The procession continued onward, everyone attached by belts, some singing. Mitrā hummed along and as time went by was mesmerized by the ritual walk.

In stark contrast to the slow-moving procession, one stationary figure caught her eye — a man on horseback by the side of the road. She started, her stomach turning in revulsion. It was the man from Kermān, both eyes fixed on her. He spat onto the ground, still staring. Mitrā faced forward, sparing just one glance in his direction, sensing tension in the crowd. Vandalism at the Towers was not unheard of and the men were prepared for any disruption. But the man did not move and she did not look at him again. The whole procession passed him by without another glance.

They arrived at the Towers and the bearers disappeared inside. Sindokht had told Mitrā and Jeren that the bearers would place the body on a stone slab and cut the shroud open. Although she couldn't see the men preparing the body for the vultures, Mitrā shivered. People waiting outside the Towers spoke words of comfort to the soul, knowing it would stay nearby for three days.

Once all that was done, everyone went home. The following three days were spent doing things that would comfort the soul. Sindokht cooked Goshtāsp's favourite dishes and fed them to Rafiq, who they believed had the ability to convey the offering to the spirit of the dead. She made an elaborate dish they rarely ate since it involved using the lining of a sheep's stomach and they didn't keep sheep. For this occasion a neighbour brought them the stomach lining and some meat from one of his own sheep. Sindokht added the meat to her black-eyed peas, onions and spices, wrapped the whole thing in the sheep's stomach and let it simmer over the fire.

It was always a family member who fed special foods to the dog. On the second day though, Sindokht passed food to Mitrā, who continued to visit. "Will you do this, my dear?"

Ābtin sat with *Amu* Bābak, who was now welcome in the home. Out of nowhere he asked the older man, "Do we have mystics, as Muslims have Sufis?"

"Not so much, son. For us, mysticism is not set apart from daily life. Some say the mystics are those who can connect with the ancient heroes sleeping in caves, the heroes who protect us from evil. Others say the prophet Zoroaster himself had that kind of vision. You see it in his poetry. Beauty is always a reminder of divine glory. Every true artist is a mystic. That's what they mean by having the artist's breath. You are one. Your father recognized your talent and didn't like it because it brought up painful memories for him. But he grew to accept and love you."

Ābtin nodded. It hadn't happened all at once but what Bābak said was true.

"Do you know about his brother? It all started with him. He was a brilliant artist, took after their mother, but he was not at all practical. Everyone was shocked when he converted to Islam and then became a Sufi. Gave up carpet weaving altogether. Goshtāsp was talented indeed. He didn't understand his own brilliance though, his skills were so different from his brother's. Perfectionist, as you've noticed. He was afraid you'd be like his brother. Terrified you'd convert."

On the third day they cleaned the house thoroughly. Another religious service took place. At this point, as the only son, Ābtin was recognized as *pol gozār*, the one who would help his father over the bridge to the next world, aided by the family dog Rafiq. There would be other ceremonies in the coming months and years. Of course Ābtin would inherit the shops and the house on the condition that his mother would continue to live there for the rest of her life. It struck him in one of those odd moments that this would curtail any ideas he might have about further travel. Unless Sindokht went with them.

At dawn on the fourth day the soul of the departed began its ascent, arriving at the bridge just as the sun's rays hit the earth. There was a moment of silence among those who gathered to see the soul off. Dogs stood by to protect the soul from evil beings lurking there, waiting to steal the passing soul. It was the time of judgment. Once past this spot, the soul continued on its way alone and the family returned to normal life.

Even though he had been handling the business for some weeks, it was hard for Ābtin to get used to the idea that he was really in charge now — permanently. One afternoon not long afterward, he met with Mitrā. "This changes everything," he told her. "I don't see how I can consider travel and I can't convert."

Mitrā couldn't help it, she cringed, tears filling her eyes. Would this mean the end?

"I do love you," he said quickly, "and am not giving up on our love. I just don't know what to do. I'm the head of my family now."

She breathed a little more easily. They sat quietly.

Finally Mitrā took a deep breath and said, "We want to be together. You're the head of your family and I'm committed to mine. You won't convert and I don't want you to. But I don't know what I'd do if it didn't work out between us. I don't want to marry anyone else."

"Nor do I," he replied, somehow acknowledging that his family would expect him to marry a Zoroastrian.

"We don't see the way now, but we can't give up, Ābtin. Something completely unexpected could happen. Throw an apple in the air and by the time it comes down to earth, the wheel has turned a thousand times."

He nodded, although in the pit of his stomach he felt that was impossible.

The green carpet was finally finished. The customer was pleased and paid the remaining money owed with a bonus for the work being completed under difficult circumstances. Now the two apprentices could work full time, helping Ābtin on his carpet, knotting while Ābtin called the colours. Rudābeh and Katayun helped with the knotting. Mitrā often sang to them as they worked. More than once, she had been followed to the village.

Everyone was worried about her safety.

14
Māhān
Late Summer 1664

Mitrā's parents wanted to remove her from the public eye for a while for her own safety and with the hope she would get some perspective on Ābtin. They decided to make a pilgrimage to the shrine of Sufi master Shah Ne'matollah Vali in the small city of Māhān, not far from Kermān in the southeast. It had been years since they were last there.

It would not have been safe to travel without a caravan, so they signed on with a group that included some of their friends and relatives. The caravan provided guards in case of attack by bandits but there was no need for a guide since the road was well-travelled and their caravan master knew it well.

The trip took eight days, stopping overnight at caravanserais, which were always located near a well or a spring. The weather was still hot, so they started very early each morning and stopped early in the afternoon. Mahmood enjoyed helping with the camels. True, horses were his favourite animals but camels would do in a pinch.

The first couple of days, the land was flat with hints of jagged mountain peaks in the distance. After the halfway point, the mountains came closer on the right side of the road, starting with gentle slopes and gradually growing to rocky peaks. On the other side of the road, the *sahrā* spread into the distance. Evenings were full of good food and music.

During the long days, the women rode sitting in enclosed seats called *kajāveh* on the camels' backs. Usually there was one woman per camel but Mitrā and Shirin shared theirs. As they rocked to and fro, Mitrā had plenty of time to think about her life.

Shirin broke the silence one afternoon. "When you marry Ābtin, where will you live?"

"I don't even know if we will marry," Mitrā groaned. "Which of us would need to give up some portion of who we are? You know that such a marriage is forbidden by both our religions."

"Surely there must be a way. Somebody must have done it before. And if they haven't, you could be the first! You know that saying? 'From this pillar to that pillar there is a space of possibility.' Remember? The story was about a man who was tied to a pillar to be executed. He asked to be tied to a different pillar and during the time that took, word came that he was not guilty of the crime he had been accused of. The man was set free. It all happened in that little space of time. Something could happen for you too."

"What if our families never reconcile to the idea?" Mitrā liked the story but wanted to stick to the point. "Could we still make a life? Living without our family is unthinkable and yet it's equally hard to think of living without Ābtin. Besides that, there are different customs to adapt to. It goes around and around in my head. Should we go to India and never see any of you again? Or stay here and never marry at all?"

She had waited so long. Now that she knew him better, she loved him even more deeply. But he would not convert to Islam, nor would she want him to — and no one was allowed to convert to Zoroastrianism. Shirin was an optimist. True, someday everything might change but it would take a miracle, and they were not saints. Why should such a thing happen for them?

At one stop, a man left the caravan to take a smaller road south through the mountains. He was going to Meymand, a village composed of a huge succession of caves that had been inhabited for thousands of years. The man had his own donkey and was on his way home. The night before he left, he spoke about the place.

"It's over on the other side of these mountains, where there are low ridges, trees and springs. Zoroastrian nomads settled in Meymand and, before our time, there were people who worshipped the sun. We have our own language, very ancient."

Shirin wished she could see the caves and thought about that odd dugout spot she had seen in the *sahrā* near Yazd. Not a cave, but still underground. There was such a bad feeling to it, not like a place where people lived or heroes slept.

Mitrā asked if the language was similar to Dari.

"Not really," the man replied. "We have a lot of words that haven't been used in Farsi since the Arabs invaded and Farsi picked up some of their words. Of course Dari doesn't have the Arabic words either. It's just that our dialects have developed differently."

Jeren also yearned to go down that road. She had heard that Meymand was rich in healing plants but knew it was too far off their route. The man said he would be riding for several days through the mountains to get there. Few people lived along that road but there were a couple of farms located on the single creek, whose pure water flowed down from the mountains.

Mitrā had never heard of Zoroastrian nomads. She wondered what it would be like to live in a cave and why anyone would choose to do so. The man said many of the caves were man-made and quite comfortable. On the other hand, how comfortable could they be with no windows, even if that gave the people protection? She was less fearful of being underground than she had been before the *qanāt* collapse, but still, it would be creepy.

Shirin pointed out that it was a good way to make a home if you lived in a place where building materials were hard to get. Caves made Mitrā think of secrets and captivity. Both of them thought the Kermāni used a cave as a hideout, maybe the place Shirin had discovered. It made Mitrā shudder to think he might have been nearby and seen her sister there.

Then an idea struck her.

"What do you think, Shirin? What if our familiarity with the *sahrā* is the whole reason he made such efforts first to connect with our family and later to discredit us. He could be afraid we'll reveal his secrets."

"Could be. I wouldn't put it past him."

Mitrā told her sister about the pilgrimage site Ābtin had been to. "There's a huge cave there where ancient heroes like the ones we hear about in the *Shāhnāmeh* are sleeping. Zoroastrians say they'll wake up when the final battle between good and evil comes. I sure hope that will be soon! Thieves and heroes, both in caves — and may the good win."

As dawn brought long shadows to the land and rosy pink and violet stripes to the sky, the girls watched from behind the curtain of the *kajāveh*. The man and his donkey disappeared into the hills. Days passed now with little more than the rhythm of camels' footsteps and the clanging of their bells. There were still mountains on their right, while on the other side the endless *sahrā* now boasted occasional well-irrigated pistachio orchards.

They arrived in Māhān toward evening on the eighth day and went directly to the public bath to wash away the dust from the road. Everyone put on clean clothes, kept carefully for this moment, and walked to the shrine surrounded by luxuriant trees. A full moon shone over high walls.

They walked in through the gate and stopped, stunned by the breathtaking beauty of the fountains and pools, the cypress trees and the shrine itself, with its magnificent dome. Students of the Sufi master sat on stone benches, reading and talking. There were families with children who wanted to play in the pools. That was still not allowed. Mitrā could vaguely remember being there as a child and climbing the long flight of stairs to the cupola.

The following evening, the travellers attended *samā*, a ceremony involving music and poetry. Ahmad said it was the surest way to connect with the sacred. Listening to the music, Mitrā felt completely at home. Impulsively she spoke to her father. "When people marry, surely there is no need for one person or the other to give up part of who they are. We become more rather than less."

"That depends on many things," he replied sternly. "Marriage always involves compromise and you are a dreamer."

Many of the travellers stayed longer in Māhān but several families, including Mitrā's, went on to the city of Kermān to visit relatives. Ahmad's brother Karim lived with his family not far from the centre of the city on a tree-lined street. He worked as a minor official in the city government. The family never really understood what it was that he did there.

At dinner time, Karim with his three grown children and his wife Sahar sat with their guests. Sahar had spread the heavy cloth *sofreh* on the floor and put out steaming dishes with delicious new specialties to try. The main course was *ābgusht*, made from eggplant, meat, garlic, caraway and a dairy product called *kashk*. They ate it with bread. This was different from the way they made it in Yazd but also delicious.

As they ate, Aunt Sahar asked Mitrā when she would marry. "The young men must be lined up outside your house!" she said with a laugh.

"It won't be long now." Mitrā gave her parents a questioning look.

Jeren looked at her plate while Ahmad turned to Karim and changed the subject. "What's new in Kermān? Surely there are some state secrets or interesting scandals you can reveal."

The brothers had always kept up a kind of teasing banter. "The water engineers are up to no good, as usual," Karim answered with a grin.

He went on in a more serious vein to tell about a certain local water engineer by the name of Mohammad. "He dug tunnels for thieves to hide their stolen goods in. But that's the least of it. He did something so utterly scandalous that I can't speak of it at dinner. His wife left him."

Karim cast a glance at his brother warning him not to pursue that subject now. Perhaps when they were alone he would say more about it. Now he continued with what could be said.

"What was worse was that his wife was found later, dead in a *qanāt*. Mohammad disappeared at the same time. Maybe he hid in one of his tunnels. I don't suppose he's turned up in Yazd? If he does, steer clear."

The five Yazdis looked at each other in surprise. "It's possible we've seen him already," said Ahmad. "He might have changed his name in Yazd. Rumour has it he may be helping thieves hide their goods there too. What does he look like?"

Shirin was thinking of the newly dug place she had seen in the *sahrā*. The scarf she saw there took on a frightening significance. Clearly she'd have to tell her father about it when she could get him alone.

Uncle Karim described the man as having a lanky build and harsh features. Ahmad drew a picture of the man who had come to Yazd. Everyone agreed that it could be the same one. Ahmad went on to draw the wife as described by Sahar. The woman looked surprisingly like Mitrā. Sahar was near tears as she said the woman was highly intelligent and walked tall.

Mitrā shuddered, thinking Nāder Kermāni might have wanted to ruin her as a kind of revenge on his wife. "What was her name?" she asked.

"Her name was Āzādeh. Ironic, isn't it?" said Sahar. "A woman whose name means a free spirit, murdered in a *qanāt*. She was my friend." The name rolled on Mitrā's tongue as she said a silent prayer for the woman's soul. This was the first time it really hit her that her life could be in danger.

Later Shirin took her father aside and told him what she had seen. He saw that she looked seriously shaken and put off asking what she was doing alone in the *sahrā* for another time.

"Keep this to yourself for now," he said. "I will deal with it when we get home." Like Mitrā, he was thinking that the man might want to discredit the whole family because they spent time in the *sahrā* and might uncover his criminal activities. Mitrā in particular, because she resembled his wife.

That night Mitrā had a dream. An earthquake had struck Yazd and people were running, screaming, trying to help others get out of the rubble. She was there with Ābtin and as the dream shifted, they worked and worked, bringing people out of danger to caves conveniently located nearby in the dreamscape. In waking life, the mountains were much farther away. All were working together without concern for differences of religion or class, which seemed completely natural in the dream. As natural as hiding underground in an earthquake! She woke for a few minutes, gasping for breath, and then slept again. The dream continued. Now they were building a new village in which people of both religions lived together in peace. She woke as sunlight came streaming through the window.

That same night, Ābtin was dreaming in his loft. He and Mitrā had left on a long journey, travelling with camels who behaved admirably in the dream. In real life, the camels in the caravan he travelled with had not been so obliging. The two were determined to make a new life in another place, one free of superstition, religious differences and family arguments. They came to a place on a hillside overlooking a river that runs year-round and lived there in peace.

Ābtin woke up with a smile on his face. Then reality seeped in. He remembered his obligations as head of the family and carrier of both the business and the art. Not to mention his love of home. He knew Mitrā shared that feeling. They would need to create that peaceful place here, in Yazd and the villages.

Mitrā and her family rejoined their group for the return journey. On the way, she had a long conversation with her parents. They said they would agree to her marrying Ābtin as long as he could support her, but only after they had got rid of the Kermāni so that Mitrā could safely walk the streets. There was no evidence of his having committed a crime in Yazd, unless the two thugs had made a statement against him. But perhaps he could be sent back to Kermān on the charge of murdering his wife. Surely that possibility would be enough to make him leave Yazd.

Still, there was more to the question of Mitrā and Ābtin's marriage than the parents' agreement. They looked at options that could be legally pursued. There was only one. He would have to convert to Islam. Less legally, the two could move together to India, as many Zoroastrians were doing to avoid the increasing levels of persecution in Iran.

"But we would so hate to lose our daughter," Jeren whispered. "Quite possibly we would never see you again."

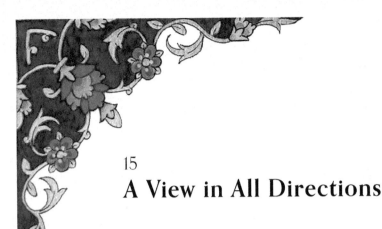

15

A View in All Directions

Ābtin came to the final day. The apprentices had knotted the last rows of the border. At last, the carpet was done. He sat down in shock while Bizhan laughed and ran to the house to get him a drink of water. Sindokht and the girls came back with him.

Ābtin made a great show of taking the knife in hand and cutting the rug from the loom, being careful to leave enough of the warp on each end to form the fringes. Everyone helped make the long threads into tassels and, when that was done, they carried the carpet to the door and laid it out in the sun. The colours shone like jewels in the bright sunshine.

As they gazed at it Ābtin said, "I tried to put everything I had seen into it — the peacocks, tigers, saffron flowers and marble mountains. And to convey the kindness of the caravan master, carpet seller, old woman and the fishermen. I wanted to send a blessing to the blind children and to all of you.

"When my father made me weave the cypress over and over, I found it boring, just a stylized image. And yet, by the time it found its place in the carpet, the image had become as real as the ancient cypress tree in Cham. Just as the desert, mountains and sea had come alive for me when I spent time with them — sometimes struggling to survive."

"And you've done it!" Sindokht exclaimed.

She and the girls rushed back to the house and returned with tea and special cookies. They had baked Ābtin's favourites, knowing that today would be the day.

"Let us be the first to sit on it!" Sindokht called. They each chose a place and admired one section closely. Bizhan sat down next to Rudābeh and smiled. They all ate, drank and sang songs as the rosy sun slipped behind the golden hills.

Mitrā's family arrived home from their trip in the evening. The next morning Ahmad went directly to the police and took them to investigate the tunnel his daughter Shirin had told him about. They found it full of stolen goods. One policeman hid nearby and waited while the other promised to replace him if he hadn't come back with the culprits by mid-afternoon.

Next, Ahmad went home and changed his dusty clothes for clean ones, washed his face and hands, and went to see the Sheikh. After the usual *ta'arof* and tea drinking, he came to the point.

"Is it ever possible to make an exception to the law saying Muslim women may not marry men of other religions? I ask on behalf of my daughter Mitrā, who is a very fine young woman, if I may say so. She does much community service and is kind to all. Mitrā is in love with a Zoroastrian, an excellent young carpet weaver. My wife and I have thought long and hard about this, and we see no reason for them not to marry. Except of course for the law. Our own experience is of a Sunni-Shia marriage and, although unconventional, it has been a very good one for many years now. My wife believes it is their destiny to bring peace to the communities and help stem the tide of violence that seems to be increasing."

The Sheikh nodded thoughtfully. "You speak well," he said. "But we cannot make exceptions. We must carry the Muslim lineage forward."

"With all due respect, my daughter says that if she cannot marry this young man she will not marry anyone. We cannot force her. If that is the case, she will not be carrying the lineage forward anyway."

"She's young." The Sheikh smiled. "She'll see it differently in a year or so. *Agha* Ahmad, I appreciate your kindness and that of your family. As you know, I oppose all violence and disrespect toward those of other religions but I will not go against the law."

Ahmad left disappointed but not defeated. After all, he had not expected immediate agreement.

After hardly sleeping a wink, Mitrā grabbed her sister right after breakfast. "Come with me to the bazaar. I've got to tell Ābtin."

Shirin was happy to go with her, practically running. If Mitrā finally married Ābtin, she would be able to marry her sweetheart Ali from the *ājil* shop. He wanted to set a date, although Shirin was not supposed to marry before her older sister.

Ābtin was talking with a customer when they arrived. The sisters tried not to look too impatient, examining various carpets, cushions and the tasseled decorative pieces people hung over their doors. After a short time, the customer caught on. "Please serve the ladies," he said. "I will return in a little while."

Once he was gone, Mitrā came closer to Ābtin, suddenly shy. "They said yes! In principle, that is."

He broke into a huge smile. "Good news! My grandmother used to say that in the desert even a sip of water is a blessing. And this is more than a sip! I will go and tell my mother. How can she object if your parents have agreed?"

Now she told him the rest, about how difficult it would be. They already knew but sometimes chose to forget. There were a few things they hadn't talked about though. It would be next to impossible to find anyone in either community who would carry out the ceremony. And that would just be the beginning. There could be even more hostility and danger than before.

"It will work out. I'm sure of it," Ābtin said and told her his dream of a peaceful time and place.

She replied with her own dream and went on to tell him what they had learned about Nāder Kermāni. "My father really wants to do something to get him arrested or at least chased out of Yazd for good. It's kind of scary. I don't know what *bābā* has in mind, but I do know he's gone to the police today."

"That would be a good thing and it's about time. A lot of people would thank your father."

Only then Ābtin remembered his own big news.

"The carpet is finished. Bizhan is just binding the edges."

"*Āfarin!* Well done! After all this time, I want to see it off the loom."

"Do come. But give me a chance to talk with my mother first."

Ābtin hurried home as soon as he was able to close the shop. Sindokht was in the kitchen chatting with Manizheh, who had brought little Rostam to admire the carpet. The child was engrossed in crawling its length and breadth, following the patterns with his fingers.

"It's beautiful, Ābtin," Manizheh said. "You look so happy."

"Not just about the carpet," he replied and turned to his mother. "Mitrā's parents have given their consent, as long as I can support her, and once Nāder has either left Yazd or been arrested. They learned bad things about him in Kermān. He is really dangerous and it's pretty certain he's working here with thieves. Mitrā's father has gone to the police."

Sindokht sighed. "There's still no proof of who attacked Rudābeh."

"Many feel sure Nāder was one of the three men," Ābtin replied.

"Nonetheless, if it went to court, it would be her word against the three of them. She would lose." They all fell silent.

Manizheh was the first to speak. "Mitrā is an extraordinary girl, Sindokht. They are clearly meant for each other. There's no real reason to object. She's not like the others. She has learned to fit in with us and even learned some Dari from Rostam. You love her yourself — I've seen it. Our village dogs love her too."

"Truly, how can calling another human unclean be a good thought or good speech?" Sindokht replied. "It certainly leads to bad action. It's something I've never understood in our religion, or in theirs. But think. Where would they live? Would she come here? He couldn't go there without converting. Who would perform the ceremony? It's never happened here before that I'm aware of."

Ābtin held his breath.

"All right, I agree. She has won my heart as well as yours. But I have no idea how it can work."

Mitrā never did find out what her father would have done to get Nāder out of town if it came to that. Instead, the opportunity fell into her lap. She was on her way home and had cut through the bazaar, stopping to enjoy some especially artful bargaining. Suddenly there he was, right beside her. She hoped he wouldn't recognize her and even hunched forward a bit to disguise her usual straight posture.

It was too late for subterfuge. He came closer and whispered in her ear, "Witch. Godless one. Have you no shame? We know what to do with the likes of you — and your friends."

She knew the best thing to do was to ignore him but suddenly she could stand it no longer. What he said was ridiculous and scary now that she knew what she did. After all, he had killed his wife. Now he seemed to be admitting to having attacked Rudābeh.

Anger overcame fear. "You have no right to make accusations, Mohammad!"

He blanched.

"Oh yes, we know all about you. Even your real name. If you think I'm so bad, then what will happen when the whole world knows what happened to Āzādeh?"

He stepped back as if the name were a slap in the face. People were gathering, attracted by the oddity of a woman shouting at a man.

"Āzādeh was his wife," Mitra addressed the growing crowd. "She was found dead in a *qanāt* in Kermān, after she left him because of his sinful behaviour. Now he has the nerve to accuse an honest Yazdi woman. Everyone knows, Mohammad. You thought no one knew your real name or your real story. You were wrong. Even the police know it now and have found your hiding place in the *sahrā*. Get out of this city while you still can and never come back."

By now, some of the men were giving the Kermāni dark looks and circling nearer. One of them was holding a strong stick, and another looked as if his fists would suffice. Several woman took Mitrā by the arms and pulled her away from the crowd.

Mohammad Kermāni broke away and ran, disappearing in the bazaar's maze of corridors. Later, word went around. A great number of shop owners had seen him pushing shoppers and sweating profusely as he ran. Putting all the gossip together piece by piece, it seemed he had gone by a circuitous route back to his lodgings, re-emerged carrying a bag and headed out of the city to the northeast. People in all quarters kept an eye out for him in case he came back, although he would have to be a fool to do that.

Later that day, Mitrā heard from her friend Haideh that two thieves had been arrested and taken to the judge. They were caught bringing valuable stolen goods into their underground hiding place and were sentenced to time in prison. They did not disclose the name of their confederate, saying they didn't know him and that he was from out of town. All the same, everyone felt they knew who the third man was and that he was gone, most

137

likely for good. As weeks went by, Mitrā and her family began to relax and regain a sense of safety.

The Sheikh's extensive network reported all of this to him. He felt gratitude to Ahmad for helping bring the thieves to justice and wished he could help the young people. But no, it would create a dangerous precedent and the daughter was an unknown quantity. True, she did community service but she was also disobedient and independent. Standing up to that Kermāni was courageous but unseemly. She should have called her father or her brother. She was known to consort with Sufis whom the government was always trying to do away with. And yet, she was appealing. A girl who needed to be returned to the fold, but not by force.

While the drama was played out in the bazaar, Ābtin's mother Sindokht dressed in her best and went to the Dastur, the priest who had sat with her husband when he was dying and administered his last rites. She was shown in and bowed deeply before him.

The Dastur spoke to her politely, asking about the family and even the dogs. At last after drinking tea and more polite conversation, he asked how he might serve her.

"I have good news and also a difficult situation," said Sindokht. "My son is doing an excellent job of taking on his father's business. In addition, Ābtin has just completed his first carpet with imagery showing his great journey. Mount Damāvand is at the heart of it. " She went silent, not sure how to go on.

He helped by asking, "Have you plans for your son's marriage?"

"We always hoped Ābtin would marry one of our neighbours. But ... he has a different desire."

"The Muslim girl?"

"Yes. He says he will marry her and no other. What am I to do?"

"Of course he knows we do not marry outside our faith."

"He has always been a good Zoroastrian. He is initiated, prays regularly and keeps to the precepts. Sadly, in this matter of marriage he is unmovable."

"And her family?"

"They have given their consent in principle, although they see the problems as clearly as we do. The girl is equally as adamant as he is and her parents appreciate his good qualities. Beyond that, I am told that her mother believes they have a destiny together — that of bringing peace to our neighbourhoods."

"And you, madam? Do you believe this?"

"In spite of some risk to herself, she has come into our community and offered much help, with her mother's medicines, her own singing and good nature. You yourself saw how helpful she was when my husband was passing, God rest his soul. This girl has helped my young nephew regain his health, learned much of our Dari language and even our village dogs now love her. She is a good person and so is my son. He welcomes Muslims who come to the shop, beyond the demands of ordinary courtesy. If anything can bring us all closer, surely young love and courageous behaviour like theirs will play a role in it. I agree. This is destiny."

"You speak eloquently, *khanom*. Your thoughts, words and deeds are good. I believe we must follow what we know in our hearts is right. At the same time, the idea of marriage between a Zoroastrian and a Muslim goes against our internal laws. Think of it this way. Our people are converting, dying and leaving the country in such numbers that of course we wish to see young people remain with us and give us more Zoroastrian children. I will need to discuss this with others." He shifted in his seat. "Will you have more tea?"

Clearly he was finished speaking for today. Sindokht accepted tea politely and took her leave as soon as was decent. She felt good about their conversation but there was no telling what the other priests would say.

Meanwhile, life went on. Mitrā was gradually getting more accepted in the village. Manizheh told those who didn't already know about the ways Mitrā had helped little Rostam and had sat with the dying Goshtāsp. Neighbours were amazed that Mitrā had learned so much Dari. Although not completely different from Farsi, Dari could be difficult for others to understand. Haideh had learned some of the language too, so she could talk with her relatives. Now the two friends could speak with each other secretly, in code.

Mitrā taught some of the village girls what she knew about medicinal plants. Rudābeh was especially interested. As for Ābtin, he began work on his next carpet, using mainly images and colours from nature.

One day Jeren and Mitrā were working together.

"You know what?" Jeren said. "Our family and Ābtin's could plan a Noruz party together. After all, both Zoroastrians and Muslims celebrate the New Year holiday."

"I'll tell Ābtin and he can talk about it with his mother."

When she heard about the idea, Sindokht agreed. They all tried to think of a place they could meet to discuss it. A place that would not be in either of their homes or neighbourhoods, such as the bazaar or the main square. In the end, they agreed to meet outdoors in the *sahrā* beyond the village. Mitrā and Jeren came on horseback and Sindokht arrived on foot with her daughters and the family dog.

They gazed out into the valley where the *qanāt* had collapsed. A gentle breeze was blowing and an eagle sailed overhead. Clouds had taken dramatic forms that day, resembling everything from a large rabbit to a new range of mountains in the heavens. Silence reigned among the women, at first uneasy, and then as it continued, companionable.

Sindokht spoke first. "We could have it right here."

"Or how about just up that hill, where we can see in all directions?" asked Jeren. "It would be a good symbol for the future — always being able to look in all directions."

They climbed the hill and sat on a large flat rock, a vantage point that offered a majestic view of the cypress tree in Cham village and jagged brown rocky hills that gave way to snow-capped mountains. Turning slowly, they admired the distant city with its warm brown walls, the shining domes of the *āb anbār* and the mosques. The air was full of the aromas of *sahrā* grasses.

Sindokht smiled. Now conversation turned to practicalities. They would bring carpets to sit on, light fires and organize festive food. All would be invited to eat food prepared by a team headed by Ābtin's and Mitrā's sisters. Those who would not agree to eat each other's food could cook their own.

The women decided on a day during the two-week holiday season and made their way back to town, walking together beside the horse. Rafiq circled around them, stopping here and there to investigate new smells.

Time passed. Summer turned to fall, and fall to winter. Mitrā attended *zikr* regularly and memorized poems by Hāfez and other poets. She sang at *samā*, visited with her family and old friends in Yazd, as well as new friends in the village. Determined to become a bridge, she invited them all to the spring Noruz party.

Ābtin continued with his weaving and enlarged the shop, employing several new workers. He wanted to be a fair employer, insisting that children only do certain jobs in his shop and only for short periods of time. He knew that their families needed extra money but insisted that children should not be abused in the workplace. After meeting the blind children begging on his journey, he realized that his father had been careful not to cause such suffering. He could admire that and he wanted to continue that part of Goshtāsp's legacy.

One morning at the beginning of the two-week Noruz holiday, the Sheikh awoke from a powerful dream, sweating and gasping for breath. No dream of this magnitude had struck him for many years. Not since dreaming that he must become a clergyman.

In the dream a storm raged, with bright rays of sunshine flashing through menacing black clouds. Rain and hail pounded the land. Thunder echoed from the rocky mountains. Boulders tumbled down. Then from inside a cave, he heard a rich and powerful voice singing a wedding song. The *moqanni's* daughter appeared with the young Zoroastrian that Ahmad had been sitting with at the coffee house. This was their wedding.

The scene shifted. Yazd was shining through the relentless rain. The *sahrā* flourished, a vibrant green. Water flowed abundantly in the *qanāts*.

The Sheikh woke up as the call to prayer rang out from the minarets of the Friday Mosque. Instead of going to the mosque, he washed and prayed in his own room. He needed to be alone. This was an important dream and it seemed to portend something wonderful, although he could not yet see what it was.

He prayed for guidance. Was this dream sent from God, indicating that he should allow the marriage between the Zoroastrian man and the Muslim woman? Or had it arisen from his own desires or even from the devil? He shuddered to think it might have come from his own desire to exercise power — even to compete with God. He continued to pray.

Noruz 1665

The day arrived. People congregated outdoors on the hilltop chosen months ago by the two families. A view opened in all directions: to the city, the village, the snow-capped mountains and the roads offering the promise of tantalizing new experiences. Most of the Zoroastrian villagers came, as well as Mitrā's relatives and family friends, and a whole contingent of Sufis. Many were surprised that they recognized each other but had never socialized together before. Guests brought plentiful dried dates, apples and figs from their own trees to augment the meal prepared by Rudābeh, Katayun and Shirin. Zoroastrians brought wine. Some tasted the food of others. The Sufi teacher was seen laughing and singing children's songs with the Zoroastrian priest. There was music, poetry reading and a whirling dervish.

Everyone knew they were celebrating more than the New Year. They were honouring new friendships and youthful love. Sindokht and Jeren wished the picnic were officially an engagement party. Most recognized that it was, in spirit.

While it was still light, Mitrā and Ābtin walked a little distance from the crowd. They gazed down at the *āb anbār*, glowing in the sunshine. So much had happened since they first met.

"I felt so clumsy when I bumped your water container."

"Something big was happening. I don't know how to say it."

She laughed. "Weave it into a carpet."

"I will do that. You know, don't you, that a Zoroastrian's promise is as good as the act. You have my promise. Nothing will separate us now."

"As you have mine."

Now Mitrā told Ābtin about her father's visit with the Sheikh. All Ahmad had told her was that the Sheikh refused to make an exception. Neither Mitrā nor her father was willing to give up though.

"What if we go ourselves? He will see that we are working for the good of all, not just for ourselves. We could convince him. We could go see the Zoroastrian priest as well."

"We can only try." Ābtin smiled. "Let's go tomorrow!"

They turned toward the Towers of Silence. No vultures were circling that day. "Maybe we'll go on a trip together some day. So you can see what is beyond the mountains. We'll walk over the bridge with thirty-three arches and drink tea in the Image of the World Square. I'll show you the amazing carpet of trees at the mountaintop and the ever-changing Caspian Sea. Or perhaps we'll go to India.

"For now, we are home."

In the late nineteenth century, the heavy taxation and professional restrictions on Zoroastrians were at last lifted in Iran. Sometime soon after 1925, the rule of Iranian law was extended to cover Zoroastrians as well as the Muslim population, who were in the majority. Zoroastrians blossomed under new educational systems and excelled in many professions.

Nowadays people do intermarry — at least those who have emigrated from Iran to other countries. For the marriage to be legal in Iran, a Zoroastrian man still must convert. Whether or not Mitrā and Ābtin married, they were ahead of their time, heroes in the long lineage of their own literature and tradition.

Information section

As I started to write, questions came up. Some were answered by knowledgeable Persian friends, and others through written sources. Most involved either the historical background, both social and political, or the two main religions that play a strong role in the story.

First, a few words about the place names Persia and Iran. It is often thought that Persia is the older of the two. That is not so. Iran was named after a character in the *Shāhnāmeh*, who settled the land that is now Iran. The name has been used since ancient times. Persia is a name given later by Europeans and its linguistic source is Pārs, a province in south-central Iran that was home to governments of the past. Now both names are used almost interchangeably in English. It seems to me that most native speakers call themselves Iranian when they refer to the country of their origin and Persian to refer to their language and culture.

Historical background

It's important to remember that Iranians are not Arabs. The ancestors of most Iranians were tribal Indo-Europeans who came from the northeast during the second millennium BCE. Later, they split into two groups: the Indo-Iranians who now live mainly in Iran and Afghanistan, and the Indo-Aryans who wound up mainly in India and Pakistan. Thousands of years later, the languages of these two branches still have much in common with each other and with most European languages, including English. In spite of the presence of many loan words, Farsi has nothing in common with the structure of Arabic, which belongs to the Semitic language family native to the Middle East and northern Africa.

The culture and history of Arabs and Iranians also differ. In the sixth century BCE, the Persian Empire stretched from Egypt to India. With the passage of time, the Empire was attacked by Alexander the Great and later by Mongols and various Turkic tribes. The most lasting changes came with the Arab invasion of the seventh century, shortly after the founding of Islam. Muslim Arabs were rapidly becoming a major world power, although at the time of the invasion, they were still nomadic herdsmen. By then, Iranians had lived with a sophisticated political and cultural structure for centuries. Groups with varying traditions, languages, religious beliefs and politics were living on Iranian territory. Most of them remain distinct to the present day, even though the nation has been politically unified.

I needed to decide *when* the story took place and chose the latter part of the Safavid dynasty, which ruled from 1501–1722. The dynasty was founded by Ismail, a descendent of Sufi Sheikh Safi. Ismail was best known for battling the Ottoman Empire and organizing Iran's economy.

Nomads who formerly moved seasonally were forced to settle. In the present day, they live mainly near Iran's borders. The city of Esfahān was transformed into a cosmopolitan capital, renowned for artistic masterpieces, including miniature painting and brilliant tilework. Iran's first printing press arrived in Esfahān at this time and coffee houses became popular. Trade and agriculture flourished and Shia Islam widely replaced Sunni.

I chose this time period because in the centuries following the Safavid dynasty, the position of Zoroastrians grew significantly more problematic and only improved in the twentieth century. I wanted my story to take place when it was still possible for Zoroastrians and Muslims to get along fairly easily, and yet far enough in the past for other elements of the plot to work. Nowadays many Zoroastrians and Muslims cherish warm friendships, whereas in earlier centuries, this was not the case.

Religions

Aspects of the story revolve around two major contrasting religions, Zoroastrianism and Islam. Other religions have also been well-represented in Iran, including Judaism and Christianity. However, before the arrival of Islam in the seventh century, most Iranians were Zoroastrians. The majority converted to Islam under Arab rule or later.

First to convert were regional rulers who were trying to maintain their own power. Others followed their lead either by choice or by force. For women who converted, life became more restrictive; they had previously been active in public life and even in military action. Thus in our story, we see that Mitrā's family is unusual although not unique, and that Turkmen and Zoroastrian women had certain freedoms in their own communities that Muslim women ordinarily did not.

Today many Iranian women have a higher education and professional standing. From the beginning of Islam, women have had the right to own property and do with it what they like, whereas in Europe and North America such rights were granted much more recently.

Zoroastrians and Muslims have much in common, including monotheism, pilgrimage and aspects of their prayer lives. In Iran, Islam adopted features of Zoroastrian religion, architecture and art. Besides their religious customs, both groups have always cultivated strong traditions of hospitality, generosity, polite speech (*ta'arof* in Farsi) and the importance of family that is shared throughout the Middle East and beyond.

In spite of these commonalities and the fact that most Iranian Muslims are descended from Zoroastrians, the latter underwent countless difficulties under the new religious authority. They were severely pressured to convert as a result of early Arab efforts to bring their conquered people to Islam. These efforts were similar to those of most conquering and colonizing nations throughout the ages. Repressive laws and steep taxation restricted Zoroastrians' activities and, in some time periods, even their clothing. Naturally this resulted in suspicion and mistrust.

As centuries passed, Zoroastrians encountered sporadic violence at the hands of local criminals, and from other Muslims who simply followed the crowd. Everything from catcalls to vandalism and sometimes physical violence became common in Zoroastrian life.

In spite of this, Zoroastrians were much appreciated for their honesty and considered good employees. Friendships and business relationships were maintained with local Muslims, some may have been relatives who had converted. However a Muslim woman has never been allowed to marry a Zoroastrian man unless he converted, while a Muslim man has been allowed to marry a woman of another religion. Because the lineage went down through the male line, the mother's religion was considered less important by those whose goal was to increase the number of Muslims.

The Arabic Caliphates did not reign long in Iran although their influence was long-lasting. By 820, Iranian groups were taking over in various parts of the country. Dynasties came and went but the efforts on the part of religious and political authorities to convert the whole population to Islam continued.

Zoroastrianism

Founded by the prophet Zoroaster (aka Zarathustra) around 1500 BCE, Zoroastrianism was Iran's state religion from shortly before 500 BCE until the arrival of Islam. It emerged from earlier animistic beliefs and became the world's first religion to be based on the revelations of a prophet. Zoroastrians worship one God, Ahura Mazda, although other life-giving immortals are also honoured. For example, while fire was revered as a deity in earlier centuries, under Zoroastrianism it is appreciated as a potent means of purification and an aid to concentration in prayer.

Zoroastrianism is highly dualistic. The all-knowing Ahura Mazda upholds the cosmic order. He is in constant conflict with the dark and evil Angra Mainyu, who emerges from evil thought and leads legions of demons and *jinns*. It is believed that the conflict between good and evil will come to a head at the end of the world and that good will prevail. There are some clear parallels with Christianity, which was influenced in early times by Zoroastrianism. For example, both religions speak of a saviour born of a virgin, who will lead humanity in the last battle against evil.

To support victory of the good, Zoroastrians adhere strictly to rules of ethical and ecological living, and honest dealings. The three major tenets are "good thoughts, good words and good deeds." Celebrations frequently take place outdoors in the mountains. There are high priests in Zoroastrianism but no central authority. Religious practice relies on an intuitive sense of rightness as well as sacred texts including the Avesta and Gathas.

Today most Iranians celebrate a number of holidays that date back to Zoroastrian times. These are not religious holidays but cultural ones, similar to Thanksgiving in North America. The New Year, Noruz, is celebrated at the spring equinox, Yaldā at the winter solstice and Mehregān at the fall equinox.

Iran's national epic is the *Shāhnāmeh,* written by Abolqasem Ferdowsi. It runs anywhere from nine to twelve volumes in Farsi (almost 900 pages in Dick Davis's abridged translation) and contains more than fifty stories of Iranian kings, both mythical and historical. The stories come from a Zoroastrian background, including strong links with the Avesta and other sacred texts, as well as oral tradition.

Ferdowsi wrote it in verse during the eleventh century. Both families in our story love tales from the *Shāhnāmeh,* and members of Ābtin's family are named after some of the characters in them. Ferdowsi is honoured in Iran for having saved the Farsi language when many other languages were being replaced by Arabic. The *Shāhnāmeh's* essentially Zoroastrian stories and their values are mainstays of Persian culture and identity.

After the Arab invasion, many Zoroastrians moved to India where they became known as Pārsis. They have always stayed in touch with the homeland. In more recent times, Zoroastrians, along with other Iranians, have emigrated to other countries as well.

At present, Zoroastrian culture is becoming ever more popular in Iran, where many are disillusioned by their Islamic government and identify with the culture of an earlier time as being more truly their own.

Islam

Islam was founded by the prophet Mohammad in the Arabian cities of Mecca and Medina in what is now Saudi Arabia. Soon after its founding in the early seventh century, Islam spread throughout the Middle East and to North Africa, India, China and beyond. Chronologically, Islam is the third monotheistic religion to emerge in the region. Judaism, Christianity, and Islam all descend from a common ancestor, the patriarch Abraham. Muslims also honour Jesus and Moses as some of the great prophets.

Prophet Mohammad's words embody understanding of a God who is compassionate and merciful to believers. The prophet stressed building a just community whose members, including women, are treated with respect, although men have always held superior legal status. Muslims rely on the prophet's revelations as passed down through the Koran and other texts, which have become guidebooks for living. There have been numerous interpretations of the Koran, as there are with sacred texts of other religions. Beyond that, there is no centralized authority in Islam.

Throughout the ages, Muslims have contributed greatly to science and the arts. All knowledge is understood as a way of knowing God, who encourages his people to explore his creation thoroughly. Astronomy, geography, climate, mapping, navigation, architecture, medicine, music, art, number systems and language study — all have thrived in the hands of Muslims. Many developments in these and other fields have come to Europe and North America through Muslim scholarship and art. I encourage you to Google the many amazing contributions they have made!

Muslims are obliged to accomplish five things in life: They must acknowledge that there is one God and that Mohammad is his prophet/messenger, help those who are less fortunate, recite five daily prayers (Shia Muslims often combine the five prayers into three prayer times), make the pilgrimage to Mecca (the *hajj*), if at all possible, and fast during the month of Ramadan.

From very early times, Islam has been composed of two main denominations: Sunni, with the majority of Muslims worldwide, and Shia, which includes the majority of the population in Iran, Iraq, Bahrain and Yemen, and minorities in other countries. The split emerged from a disagreement about leadership succession after the prophet's death. At the time of our story, the shift from Sunni to Shia was just happening in Iran.

152

Islam first arrived in Iran on a wave of invasion from the south that is still remembered bitterly today. It took several centuries to reach every corner of the Empire. Even in some places that had been defeated by Arab armies, the religion was slow to take hold. Pockets of Zoroastrianism survived, most notably in Yazd where their sacred flame still burns today.

Sufis

A third form of Islam that enters our story is the mystical tradition of Sufism. Sufis aspire to a direct and personal connection with God. They make this connection through meditation and by following wise teachers. Poetry and music play an important role in their practice. Sufis teach that the path is inside us, not in dogma. Experience is valued more than theory. Breaking habits is encouraged, to keep experience fresh. We should not throw out the old away, they say, just rearrange and reinterpret it. Their practices encourage an intuitive experience of love, rather than blind acceptance of doctrine.

Other forms of mysticism existed in the region before the coming of Islam. They may have influenced the early Sufis, who emerged during the earliest period of Islam. Some say the prophet's daughter Fatima was one of the first, although others disagree. In any case, there have been many female Sufis and poets. Most Sufis are Sunni, while some are Shia. Community service is a strong part of their practice.

There have been various schools of Sufism down through the centuries. Some leaders gained wealth and prestige. Others wore rags and adhered to vows of poverty. Sufis have often been marginalized and persecuted in Iran and other countries, even though Iran's Safavid dynasty was founded by Sufis.

The Sufis Mitrā and her mother meet in our story are inspired by the *madhab-e-eshq* or Path of Love, which began in the twelfth century. The Path of Love flourished in the city of Neyshabur, located in the northeast corner of today's Iran. Neyshabur was a major Islamic centre during the ninth through twelfth centuries. Among the great poets inspired by the Path of Love are Ahmad Ghazali, Farid ud-din Attar and Omar Khayam, who see passionate love as the way to God.

Zoroastrian mysticism

The Zoroastrian view of mysticism is less well-known than the Muslim view. It is widely believed that the prophet Zoroaster was a mystic, as evidenced in the sacred texts. Scholar James R. Russell says mysticism is mainly connected to the image of the heroic defeat of evil in ancient stories. Heroes are now waiting, sleeping in caves and can be contacted through prayer and ordinary life work. Beyond that, perhaps we can also consider artistic endeavours as paths of mysticism, as Ābtin's uncle advises him.

Pronunciation Guide

Most Farsi sounds are similar to those in English.

a: as in cat

ā: as the [aw] in awesome

e: as in egg

i: as the [ee] in beet

o: as in roll

u: as the [oo] in boot

g: as in good (always hard, never soft as in George)

h: as in English (h is never silent)

j: as in jolly

q: English does not have this sound. It is similar to a French r. Close your throat at the very back of your tongue. Release the breath as if pronouncing the letter k. It may sound like a slight gargle (occasionally written gh)

y: as in yet

kh: English does not have this sound. It is similar to the German ch, as in J.S. Bach

zh: as the z in azure

Glossary

āb anbār — A large water cistern. Water flows through underground channels (see qanāt) and is stored in a pool under a large dome (see also bādgir).

ābgusht — A dish eaten in Kermān, made from eggplant, meat, garlic, caraway and a dairy product called kashk. In Yazd, the recipe might include lamb on the bone, potato, chickpeas, onion and turmeric.

āfarin — Excellent! or Well done!

agha — Mr. or sir.

Ahura Mazda — The name of God in the Zoroastrian religion.

ājil — Unsalted nuts, sometimes combined with dried fruits.

amu — Paternal uncle. The title is also used affectionately, most often by children when addressing an adult male friend of the family.

Anahita — Ancient Iranian goddess of fertility, healing and wisdom. Associated with water.

ātāsh — Fire.

ātash bahrām — Zoroastrian sacred fire.

Avesta — One of the Zoroastrian sacred texts.

azān — Muslim call to prayer, heard three times daily in Iran.

aziz, azizam — Dear, My dear.

bābā — Papa.

bādgir — Wind tower used for air conditioning and keeping water fresh.

bāqlavā — Sweet dessert, similar to Greek baklava.

bebakhshid — Excuse me or Forgive me.

befarmayid — A polite way of making an invitation, such as "Come in," "After you," or "Please sit down."

chādor — A large piece of cloth, also called a veil in English, worn by Iranian women when in the presence of men who are not related to them in a limited number of ways. The chādor covers all of her hair and disguises the shape of her body. The word literally means "tent."

chāh — A well. Also an opening into a water channel, used while building and maintaining the channel.

daf — A single-headed drum with metal rings inside.

dokhtar — Daughter or girl.

Gatha — One of the Zoroastrian sacred texts.

gor — Disrespectful term for a Zoroastrian. From the Farsi *gabr*, meaning unbeliever.

hajj — The pilgrimage to Mecca, made by devout Muslims.

Inshallāh — If God wills it.

jinn — Supernatural creature in Islamic mythology and pre-Islamic Arabian mythology, made of fire and smoke.

kajāveh — Enclosed seat used by women when travelling on camels.

kamāncheh — Persian bowed string instrument.

kārvān sālār — Caravan master.

kashk — Dairy product somewhat similar to yogurt.

khanom — Madam, Mrs. or Ms.

kheili mamnun — Thank you very much.

khodā hāfez — Good-bye.

khodā rā shokr — Thank God.

koshti — Woven belt worn by Zoroastrians who have passed through their initiation.

madraseh — Elementary school or religious school.

moqānni — Master water engineer. Also a worker who builds and maintains water systems.

naqqāl — Storysinger, especially one who specializes in the *Shāhnāmeh*, Iran's greatest epic.

Noruz — New Year's holiday, celebrated for about two weeks at the spring equinox.

pardeh — Scroll that is often hung near a storysinger during a performance. May feature scenes from the story being told.

Pārs — Province in south-central Iran. It was the homeland of the Persian people and, in ancient times, the capital of Iran. Pārs is the source of the word Persia and the name of the Farsi language.

pashmak — Sweet treat similar to cotton candy. A specialty of Yazd.

pesaram — My son. From pesar, son or boy. Used affectionately.

pir — Old. Other meanings include a saint or a shrine.

pol gozār — Guardian of the bridge to the next world in the Zoroastrian tradition.

qanāt — Water channel, which usually runs underground from a source of groundwater near the base of a mountain to places where water is needed.

qotāb — A sweet dumpling. Specialty of Yazd. Plural *qotābhā*.

rushkoryak — (Dari) Hello. Used in the afternoon.

sab bukheir — (Dari) Good morning.

sahrā — Dry, barren land. Fertile if irrigated. May also refer to a desert.

salām — Hello.

samā' — Sufi spiritual concert.

Shāhnāmeh — Iran's greatest epic poem, written between 977 and 1010 by Abolqasem Ferdowsi.

shātereh — Medicinal plant useful for clearing negative energies from the home.

Sharia — Islamic religious law.

shav do khash — (Dari) Good night.

sheikh — In Shia Islam, a high-level cleric. In Sufi tradition, a teacher.

siāvshun — Medicinal plant useful for treatment of shock.

Simorgh — Mythic bird known for her wisdom and for spreading seeds. Appears several times in the Shāhnāmeh. Lives on Mount Damāvand.

soffeh — A covered place to sit, adjacent to the courtyard in many older Iranian houses.

sofreh — A cloth placed on the floor or outdoors where people sit to share meals.

Sufi — Muslim mystic.

ta'arof — Polite speech.

tār — Persian plucked stringed instrument.

termeh — Highly prized silk fabric with woven designs. Specialty of Yazd.

Towers of Silence — Towers where Zoroastrians exposed the bodies of the dead. No longer in use in Iran.

tumār — Book used by storysingers.

zikr — Remembrance of God. A Sufi gathering for meditative chanting.

Sayings

In Farsi, many sayings are commonly in use.
Here are a few that appear in our story:

Chapters 3 and 5 – Mitrā shivered, as if she had seen the angel of death. Rudābeh refers to the expression when she says, "That expression, 'a fate worse than death,' made me feel as if I had seen the angel of death."

Similar to English: She felt as if someone were walking on her grave.

Chapter 4 – Goshtāsp says, "Stupid boy, can't tell a camel from a cow."

An expression of exasperation.

Chapters 5 and 15 – When the old woman gives Ābtin water, he says, "It reminds me of the saying, 'In the desert a small sip of water is a blessing.'" In this case, it's literally true. Ābtin repeats the expression when he hears that Mitrā's parents have agreed to their marriage. This time he means, "It's a good start."

Chapter 5 – Ābtin says, "I didn't want to appear ungrateful, or as we say, one who doesn't recognize salt."

In a very dry climate, salt is essential and saves lives of both people and animals. Not to appreciate it would be the height of crudeness.

Chapter 6 – Bābak says of Mitrā's father, "He's the kind with a giving hand, not a grasping hand."

He's generous, not greedy.

Chapters 7 and 13 – Ābtin's mother tells him, "You have what they call the breath of an artist — a real inspired talent." Later, when Goshtāsp is dying, he says, "My mother was the one with the real talent, the artist's breath and technique." Bābak also refers to it.

This saying distinguishes between an artist who has brilliant technique from one who has not only technique but genuine inspiration, which is understood to be in the breath.

Chapter 7 – Ābtin is frustrated by his continuous arguments with his father and says, "He's like a bird with one foot."

He is constantly repeating the same thing, hopping on one foot and not seeing the other side of the argument.

Chapters 13 and 14 – Shirin tries to cheer Mitrā up, telling her that some small thing could change their situation and make the marriage possible. She tells the story behind the saying.

From this pillar to that pillar there is a space of possibility.

Shirin means that we should never give up.

A similar saying says:

Throw an apple in the air and by the time it comes to earth, the wheel turns a thousand times.

Suggestions for Further Reading

Amirrezvani, Anita. *Blood of Flowers*. New York: Back Bay Books, 2007.

Boyce, Mary. *Zoroastrians: Their Religious Beliefs and Practices*. New York: Routledge, 2001.

Boyce, Mary. *A Persian Stronghold of Zoroastrianism*. Oxford: Clarendon Press, 1977.

Davis, Dick, trans. *Shahnameh, The Persian Book of Kings*. New York: Penguin Books, 2007.

Friedl, Erika. *Women of Deh Koh: Lives in an Iranian Village*. New York: Penguin Books, 1991.

Ladinsky, Daniel, trans. *The Gift: Poems by Hafiz, the Great Sufi Master*. New York: Penguin Compass, 1999.

Price, Massoume. *Medieval Iran*. Vancouver: Anahita Productions, 2012. http://cultureofiran.com/index.html.

Price, Massoume. *Beauty and Fashion. History of Clothing and Jewellery in Iran*. Vancouver: Anahita Productions, 2012. http://cultureofiran.com/index.html.

Sadri, Ahmad, Hamid Rahmanian and Sheila Canby. *Shahnameh: The Epic of the Persian Kings*. New York: The Quantuck Lane Press, 2013.

Safi, Omid. "On the 'Path of Love' Towards the Divine: A Journey with Muslim Mystics." The *Journal of Scriptural Reasoning* 3, no. 2 (August 2003).

http://jsr.shanti.virginia.edu/vol-3-no-2-august-2003-healing-words-the-song-of-songs-and-the-path-of-love/on-the-path-of-love-towards-the-divine-a-journey-with-muslim-mystics/#n65

To see photos and more impressions from my journey in Iran, please visit www.kiravan.com/postcards_iran_intro.html.

Acknowledgements

Many people have given me their help and support in writing and publishing this book. My heartfelt thanks go to friends who read early drafts and engaged in fruitful conversation, to my splendid artists and those who gave permission to use their poems and translations.

Fleur Talebi and Hossein Mashreghi generously showed me around Iran, introducing me to their hospitable friends and relatives, as well as the culture and landscapes. On that trip, Fleur told me the story that mushroomed into this one, and later she helped with the writing.

For several years, Haideh Hashemi has taught me Farsi — and language always opens doors to understanding. We have also discussed details about literature and culture, including the story of Ārash.

Massoume Price has shared her expertise on social history, clothing and much more, both in our conversations and from her wonderful books. She also offered interesting plot possibilities.

Narges Govahi shared fascinating details about the storysinger and his performance, as well as the story of Ārash and the nature of his heroism.

Mahvash Aidun from Yazd showed me her mother's traditional clothing and jewellery, and later answered questions about Dari language, Yazdi food and healing plants. She brought the villages to life for me.

Shirin Shahbandari helped with foods my Zoroastrian family might have eaten.

I'm grateful to Mahdiyar Biazi and Shamin Zahabioun for our consultation about art and for their excellent work making the perfect illustrations for the book. Mahdiyar's spectacular page corners and Shamin's evocative map invite us into the story.

I rely on my community of storytellers for endless warm support. Thanks to Mariella Bertelli and others for encouraging me to expand the tale from its oral version. Support and feedback have come from Linda Stender, Liz Tanner, Jane Wintemute, Allice Bernards, Anne Andersen and Helen May. I'm also grateful to audiences coast to coast for feedback on the oral telling of Mitrā's and Ābtin's stories.

Presenters and the participants in an excellent course offered by Simon Fraser University and the Agha Khan University in 2014 have enriched my understanding of Islam and mysticism.

Thanks to the team at FriesenPress, who made the publication process a pleasure. Special thanks to Jessica Feser who guided me through the process with unfailing efficiency, patience and good humour. I'm also grateful to Davina Haisell, Gayle Friesen and one anonymous editor for their editing, which made the book so much clearer and richer. Needless to say, all mistakes are my own!

Warm thanks to the poet Daniel Ladinsky for permission to use his rendition of "Vintage Man," which inspired Ābtin on his journey. Mr. Ladinsky has introduced the work of the poet Hāfez to English language readers in a truly accessible way. I often turn to his books for guidance.

Professor Omid Safi introduced me to Sufism and generously answered my questions, especially about the Path of Love. I'm also grateful for permission to use two of his translations from the poetry of ʿAyn al-Qozat Hamadani.

Thanks also to Ahmad Sadri for permission to quote the opening words of the storysinger from his magnificent rendition of the Shāhnāmeh.

In Chapter 8, I have quoted with gratitude from Dick Davis's translation of the Shahnameh. A short rewording from *Blood of Flowers* by Anita Amirrezvani appears in Chapter 7. (See Suggestions for Further Reading.)

Permissions

Hāfez poem "Vintage Man" (Chapter 5). From the Penguin publication, *The Gift: Poems by Hafiz, the Great Sufi Master.* Copyright © 1999 Daniel Ladinsky. Used with his permission.

Shāhnāmeh opening (Chapter 8). From the Quantuck Lane Press publication, *Shahnameh: The Epic of the Persian Kings* by Ahmad Sadri, Hamid Rahmanian and Sheila Canby. Translation and adaptation copyright © 2013 Ahmad Sadri. Used with his permission.

Two poems by ʿAyn al-Qozat Hamadani, translated by Omid Safi (Chapters 11 and 12). From the *Journal of Scriptural Reasoning* article, "On the 'Path of Love' Towards the Divine: A Journey with Muslim Mystics." Poetry translation copyright © 2003 Omid Safi. Used with his permission.

About the Author

Photo by Robert D. MacNevin

Writer, oral storyteller, cellist, and Farsi-speaker, Kira Van Deusen mixes a love of music with a passion for language and research to create enchanting, human stories. She has published several nonfiction books about storytelling in Siberia and the Canadian north. *Faraj: A Space of Possibility* is her first book of fiction, inspired by a story she heard in Iran. Kira lives in Vancouver, British Columbia. Visit her website at www.kiravan.com.

"In the manner of medieval tales from the Middle East, this heartwarming romance is filled with adventure and words of wisdom. The story smoothly and unconsciously takes the reader into the exotic and unfamiliar land of Safavid Iran. This happens at a time of immense cultural and religious change, when religion not only mattered but also dictated life. Romance between a Muslim woman and a Zoroastrian man was strictly forbidden. In our own time of uncertainty, radicalism and abundance of violent dogmas, this tender tale is a fresh start into a better understanding of the hearts and minds of the the story's land and people." Massoume Price, social anthropologist and author of numerous books on Iranian culture.

CPSIA information can be obtained
at www.ICGtesting.com
Printed in the USA
LVOW06s0041020616
490528LV00011B/31/P

9 781460 286814